The Secret of Shady Glen

As Nancy struggled with Holly in the dim light, she heard Ethan jumping down from the roof.

She spun around to face him, but she'd been too slow. He grabbed her arms and flashed the knife in front of her face.

"*Don't* try anything like that again!" he said furiously. By then, Holly had gotten the lantern lit, and the whole tomb was bathed in a flickering, ghostly light.

Suddenly Nancy saw that the stone cover of the coffin was open. They couldn't really mean to put her in there!

Ethan watched Nancy stare in horror at the open coffin. "This," he said, "is going to be your new home!"

Nancy Drew
Mystery Stories

#57 The Triple Hoax
#58 The Flying Saucer Mystery
#59 The Secret in the Old Lace
#60 The Greek Symbol Mystery
#61 The Swami's Ring
#62 The Kachina Doll Mystery
#63 The Twin Dilemma
#64 Captive Witness
#65 Mystery of the Winged Lion
#66 Race Against Time
#67 The Sinister Omen
#68 The Elusive Heiress
#69 Clue in the Ancient Disguise
#70 The Broken Anchor
#71 The Silver Cobweb
#72 The Haunted Carousel
#73 Enemy Match
#74 The Mysterious Image
#75 The Emerald-eyed Cat Mystery
#76 The Eskimo's Secret
#77 The Bluebeard Room
#78 The Phantom of Venice
#79 The Double Horror of Fenley
  Place
#80 The Case of the Disappearing
  Diamonds
#81 The Mardi Gras Mystery
#82 The Clue in the Camera
#83 The Case of the Vanishing Veil
#84 The Joker's Revenge
#85 The Secret of Shady Glen
#86 The Mystery of Misty Canyon
#87 The Case of the Rising Stars

#88 The Search for Cindy Austin
#89 The Case of the Disappearing
  Deejay
#90 The Puzzle at Pineview School
#91 The Girl Who Couldn't
  Remember
#92 The Ghost of Craven Cove
#93 The Case of the Safecracker's
  Secret
#94 The Picture-Perfect Mystery
#95 The Silent Suspect
#96 The Case of the Photo Finish
#97 The Mystery at Magnolia
  Mansion
#98 The Haunting of Horse Island
#99 The Secret at Seven Rocks
#100 A Secret in Time
#101 The Mystery of the Missing
  Millionairess
#102 A Secret in the Dark
#103 The Stranger in the Shadows
#104 The Mystery of the Jade Tiger
#105 The Clue in the Antique Trunk
#106 The Case of the Artful Crime
#107 The Legend of Miner's Creek
#108 The Secret of the Tibetan
  Treasure
#109 The Mystery of the Masked
  Rider
#110 The Nutcracker Ballet Mystery
#111 The Secret at Solaire
#112 Crime in the Queen's Court
#113 The Secret Lost at Sea

Available from MINSTREL Books

85

NANCY DREW®

THE SECRET OF SHADY GLEN

CAROLYN KEENE

A MINSTREL® BOOK

PUBLISHED BY POCKET BOOKS

New York   London   Toronto   Sydney   Tokyo   Singapore

This book is a work of fiction. Names, characters, places and incidents are either the product of the author's imagination or are used fictitiously. Any resemblance to actual events or locales or persons, living or dead, is entirely coincidental.

A MINSTREL PAPERBACK *ORIGINAL*

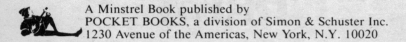

A Minstrel Book published by
POCKET BOOKS, a division of Simon & Schuster Inc.
1230 Avenue of the Americas, New York, N.Y. 10020

Copyright © 1988 by Simon & Schuster Inc.
Cover artwork copyright © 1988 by Glen Hastings

Produced by Mega-Books of New York, Inc.

ISBN: 0-671-63416-X

First Minstrel Books printing September, 1988

10 9 8 7 6 5 4 3

NANCY DREW, NANCY DREW MYSTERY STORIES, A MINSTREL BOOK and colophon are registered trademarks of Simon & Schuster Inc.

Printed in the U.S.A.

Contents

1	The Secret Drawer	1
2	Hidden Gold	13
3	At the Curious Cat	23
4	Break-in at Bess's House	35
5	The Trail of the Treasure Map	49
6	Nancy on Top of the Case	60
7	The Thieves Strike Again	68
8	A Grave Discovery	76
9	Kristin Confesses—Almost	87
10	A Startling Revelation	98
11	Nancy Sets a Trap	107
12	Buried Alive!	114
13	The Gold Is Found!	121
14	Thieves on the Run	126
15	The Police Step In	135
16	Bethany's Story	142

THE SECRET
OF SHADY GLEN

1

The Secret Drawer

"Come on," Nancy Drew said to her friend Bess Marvin. "We have to take a shortcut or we'll be late." The girls were standing on the curb a few blocks from Bess's house. It had been a hot, humid summer day. Now, at dusk, a thick fog was beginning to rise.

Nancy flipped the ends of her reddish blond hair over her shoulders and started across the foggy street.

Bess hurried after her. But when she saw where Nancy was heading, she froze in her tracks.

"Forget it," Bess said firmly. "I'm not taking any shortcut through Shady Glen Cemetery. No way."

Nancy turned to her friend. Bess was nervously playing with a lock of her long blond hair. Her light blue eyes had a frightened look in them.

"I know this fog makes the cemetery seem kind of spooky," Nancy said, "but—"

"But *nothing*," Bess interrupted. "Shady Glen is just about the creepiest place in the world." She shook her head emphatically. "I'm not going in there, and that's final!"

Nancy sighed. Bess was definitely *not* the bravest person in the world. Sometimes she could be really stubborn, too. But Nancy knew that Bess was also a loyal, caring friend.

"Look, Bess," Nancy said, "it's almost seven-thirty. If we don't take this shortcut, we're going to be late for your baby-sitting job and Joanna will miss her evening class. She's counting on you to take care of Josh tonight. I know you don't want to let her down."

"You're right," Bess admitted. "I don't want to let Joanna down. And I promised Josh I'd make cinnamon popcorn with him." She looked at Nancy. "But let's make this cemetery shortcut really *short*, okay?"

Nancy smiled and nodded. "Let's go," she said.

Bess took a deep breath and followed Nancy through the huge iron gate into the old, run-down cemetery.

"Anyway, whose idea was it to leave your car at my house and walk to Joanna's?" muttered

Bess, as she picked her way carefully down the foggy path.

"It was *your* idea," Nancy said. "Remember? You said walking was part of your new diet and exercise plan."

"Oh, right," Bess said. She stared at the ground, trying to ignore the gravestones and monuments that loomed up at them out of the mist.

Suddenly Nancy stopped short. Bess bumped into her.

"What's wrong?" Bess demanded. "Why did you stop?"

Nancy pointed across the cemetery. "Look over there," she said. "See those three people sitting on the steps of that monument? I wonder what they're doing in Shady Glen Cemetery. No one ever comes here."

"No one except us," muttered Bess, glancing uneasily at where Nancy was pointing. She breathed a huge sigh of relief when she saw that the people sitting by the monument were actually people and not ghosts.

Nancy looked hard at the threesome, trying to see if she could recognize them, but they were too far away. The fog swirled around the monument again, almost completely hiding the three people.

"Who knows what they're doing here?" Bess said nervously. "Maybe they're waiting for

3

Halloween." She grabbed Nancy's arm. "Come on. Let's get out of here."

Nancy took one last look at the threesome. Then she shrugged and said, "It's no big deal if they want to hang out in a graveyard. I guess I was just looking for a little mystery in my life. So far, this summer has been really *boring.*"

The girls threaded their way past a few old, broken tombstones. Up ahead, the fog curled around the white stone pillars of the Mortmain mausoleum. The small building looked both beautiful and spooky, half hidden in the mist.

Beyond the mausoleum, Nancy could just make out the gate at the far end of the cemetery.

"Nearly there," she said to Bess.

"Good," said Bess.

A few minutes later, the girls were walking quickly down a grassy slope toward the gate.

"Whew!" said Bess, after they had stepped through the gate and onto the sidewalk. "I'm glad that's over with!" She glanced at her watch. "We should be at Joanna's a few minutes early," she said cheerfully. "I hope she baked one of her famous blueberry pies last night."

"What about your diet?" Nancy asked with a smile.

"Give me a break," Bess replied, grinning. "Walking through graveyards makes me hungry!"

Nancy laughed and rolled her eyes. Bess thought she was slightly plump, and she was always talking about going on a diet.

"I'll start my diet tomorrow," promised Bess.

"Where have I heard that before?" Nancy asked teasingly.

The girls turned a corner onto the street where Joanna Williams and her son, Josh, lived. This part of River Heights was a development of small, modern ranch-style homes. The only house that looked different was Joanna's. It was a large white three-story house with a huge wraparound front porch. Joanna had once told Nancy and Bess that the house was over one hundred years old.

"It's too bad Joanna hasn't been able to really fix this place up," Bess said, as the girls headed up the walk. "The house could really use a coat of paint. And the garden is full of weeds."

"Give Joanna time," replied Nancy. "Remember, she hasn't been living here that long. And it's been tough on her since her husband died. She's been working full-time, going to college, and raising a kid—all on her own."

"I don't know how she does it all," Bess said, shaking her head.

They walked up the porch steps to the door. Bess lifted the polished brass rooster-shaped knocker and tapped it against the door.

A moment later, the door swung open. Nancy and Bess found themselves facing Joanna Williams, a tall, slim, attractive black woman.

"Hi, girls, come on in," Joanna said. She stepped aside to let Nancy and Bess into the house.

Joanna smiled at them warmly. But Nancy could see from the circles under her eyes that she was totally exhausted.

"I'm glad you're here," Joanna said, as she led them into the cozily furnished living room. "I have to get to class early."

"What's up?" Bess wanted to know. "Why the early start tonight?"

"I have to give an oral report in psychology class, and I'm a complete nervous wreck over it," Joanna explained. "I need to look over my notes once more before class starts. I'd hate to forget everything I'm supposed to say."

"Don't worry, I'm sure you'll be great," Nancy said, with an encouraging smile. She dropped her purse onto the chair next to an intricately made wooden rolltop desk.

"This is a beautiful desk," Nancy said admiringly. "It must be a really valuable antique."

"I don't know if it's valuable," Joanna replied, smiling. "But it's definitely old. There were a lot of old pieces of furniture in the house when we moved in. I sold a few of the pieces and kept the others, like the desk."

Joanna stepped over to the curved flight of

stairs. "Josh!" she called. "Come downstairs, please. Bess and Nancy are here."

The girls heard running feet overhead, and in a moment, five-year-old Josh Williams came bounding down the stairs, the cloth feet of his Roboman pajama suit flapping against the wooden steps. "Hi, Bess!" he shouted. He dashed up to her and gave her a huge hug.

"Hey, what about me?" Nancy said, crouching down. Josh hugged her quickly.

Then he turned to Bess and said, "Can we make cinnamon popcorn and watch a movie on TV like last time? Please?"

"Sounds good to me," Bess replied. "What's on TV that you want to watch?"

Josh's eyes lit up. *"Creeps and Sneaks,"* he said positively.

"Ooooh, too scary for me," Bess replied. "But there's a Roboman cartoon special on cable. How about that?"

"Great!" Josh scooted across the floor and dropped easily onto the sofa.

"Well, I'd better get going," Joanna said. "There's half of a blueberry pie in the kitchen, in case you get hungry. Make yourselves comfortable, and I'll see you around ten." She scooped Josh off the couch and gave him a big kiss. "Be a good boy, and listen when Bess and Nancy tell you to go to bed," she told her son. Then she grabbed a large, book-stuffed shoulder bag off the floor and started for the door.

"Bye, Joanna. Good luck with your report," Nancy called after her.

"Thanks, I think I'm going to need it," Joanna said as she unlocked the door. She turned and added, "You two be careful, and be sure to lock up after me. I haven't felt safe since all those robberies started around here."

Nancy nodded. She'd heard about the robberies that had recently taken place in Joanna's neighborhood, but she didn't think it was likely the thieves would choose the Williamses' house to break into that night. They usually picked houses that were empty.

"We'll be careful," Nancy promised. Joanna stepped outside, and in a few seconds, Nancy heard the engine on Joanna's car roar into action. Nancy closed the front door and locked it. Then she headed for the kitchen where Bess and Josh were making popcorn.

Twenty minutes later, Nancy, Bess, and Josh were munching popcorn and watching TV, when the phone rang. "I'll get it," Josh cried. He jumped off the sofa, dashed over to the rolltop desk, and picked up the receiver. "Hello?" He listened for a moment, then turned to Bess and Nancy, a serious look in his eyes. "It's Mommy," he told them. "She wants to talk to one of you."

Nancy set the bowl of popcorn on the floor and stepped to the phone. "Hi, Joanna," she said.

8

"Nancy?" Joanna said in a frantic voice. "You're not going to believe this, but I forgot to bring the notes for my oral report!"

"Oh no!" Nancy exclaimed. "That's awful!"

"You bet it is. I know how to solve the problem—but I need your help."

"Tell me what you want me to do," Nancy said promptly.

"I'd like you to read the notes to me over the phone. I'll jot down all the figures I need. Okay?"

"Fine. Just tell me where the notes are."

"In the bottom drawer of the rolltop," Joanna told her. "You'll see a small stack of index cards clipped together."

Nancy bent over, slid open the drawer, and began to rummage through it. She found a stack of old phone bills, an envelope, Joanna's physics paper from the past semester, and a handful of loose pennies, but there were no index cards. "Hold on, I'm having a little trouble finding them," Nancy said.

She checked the pigeonholes, then pulled open the two top drawers, searching quickly through each one. But she found only a few more bills and envelopes, a couple of letters, and some pencils and paper clips.

Nancy was beginning to get worried. What if the notes weren't in the desk, after all? She began to toss items out of the drawers onto the floor. She hated messing up the desk, but she promised herself she'd clean things up later. If she didn't find those notes, Joanna's whole report would be ruined, and she knew her friend had worked much too hard for that.

"Joanna, I'm still looking," she reported into the phone.

Nancy emptied out all the drawers, but she wasn't able to find Joanna's notes. She had to find them—and fast. Joanna was hanging on to the phone, counting on her help.

Nancy thrust her hand inside the top right-hand drawer, all the way to the back. Maybe the notes had gotten stuck between the back of the drawer and the desk itself.

After checking each top drawer twice and coming up empty-handed, Nancy tried the bottom drawer again. When she felt around inside it, she blinked in surprise. On the outside, that drawer was the same depth as the others. But on the inside, it was much shallower.

There could be only one explanation, Nancy reasoned. There had to be a hidden compartment inside that bottom drawer. Nancy wondered if Joanna knew it was there. She also wondered if anything was in it.

"Nancy?" she heard Joanna say. "Have you found the notes yet?"

Nancy put the hidden drawer out of her mind for the moment. She had to find those notes!

"I'm here, Joanna," she said. "And I'm still looking."

Quickly, she sorted through the pile of stuff she'd tossed on the floor. One envelope seemed to bulge more than the others. She flipped it open. There, among some old bank statements, were the missing notes. Joanna must have placed them in the envelope by accident.

"I've got them!" Nancy said into the telephone.

"Great!" replied Joanna. "For a minute there, I thought we were out of luck."

"Here we go," Nancy said, studying the first card. Carefully she reeled off the list of facts Joanna had written on the card. In another few minutes, she'd read everything Joanna needed from the stack of cards.

"You're a lifesaver," Joanna said gratefully, when Nancy had finished.

"No problem," replied Nancy. "It sounds as if it's going to be a great report." Then she added, "By the way, did you know that you have a secret compartment in your desk?"

"No, I didn't know that," Joanna said in a surprised tone. "Check out the drawer, if you want to. Now I've really got to go. Thanks a million for reading me those notes."

Nancy wished Joanna luck and hung up the phone. Then she bent over and began to examine the lower drawer of the desk. Using her own hand as a kind of rough ruler, Nancy quickly measured the drawer. It was true. On the outside, all three drawers were six inches deep. But on the inside, the bottom drawer had somehow lost two whole inches.

Nancy ran her fingers across the bottom of the drawer. Suddenly she felt a tiny hole in the wood toward the back. She pressed down on the hole. Nothing happened. Then, gently, she dug one fingernail into the little hole and pulled. There was a click; then the entire bottom of the drawer flipped up.

Nancy's eyes widened as she stared into the extra two inches of the bottom drawer.

"Bess!" she called out. "Come over here and look at this!"

2

Hidden Gold

Bess hurried over to the desk. "What is it?" she asked.

Nancy pointed to the hidden compartment. Inside, caked with dust, lay a rolled-up piece of parchment, tied neatly with a faded blue ribbon.

Bess looked at Nancy. "Well, what are we waiting for?" she said. "Let's unroll it and see what it says."

Nancy took the parchment out of the drawer and gently blew the dust off it. "I think we'd better wait for Joanna," she replied, placing the parchment on top of the desk.

"I guess you're right," Bess agreed reluctantly, eyeing the parchment. Then she looked across the room at Josh. He was standing in front of the TV, his hand on the dial. "Anyway, it's Josh's bedtime," added Bess. "I just hope I

13

can convince *him* it's time for bed." She headed over to the little boy.

Nancy began to pick up the items she'd tossed on the floor during the search for Joanna's notes.

When Joanna arrived home later that evening, Nancy handed her the rolled-up parchment. "I found it in the hidden compartment in your desk drawer," Nancy explained.

"This is amazing!" Joanna said, taking the paper. Her eyes sparkled with excitement as she looked at the rolled-up parchment. "I think this may be the solution to a mystery that's been bothering me for the past year!" She smiled at the girls. "Let's go into the kitchen and have some lemonade. Then I'll unroll the paper, and we'll see what it says."

Moments later, Nancy, Joanna, and Bess were seated at the kitchen table with tall glasses of cold lemonade. Joanna slid off the blue ribbon and unrolled the parchment. Then she spread the paper out on the table.

The three peered at the paper. "It's just a bunch of funny drawings and some lines," Bess said, frowning.

Nancy studied the paper closely. A few clumsily drawn pictures dotted the page: a skull inside a square box, a dragon breathing fire, and a rooster. Curving lines led from drawing to drawing. "I think this is a map," she said. "The pictures are probably clues, and the lines look as if they mark out some kind of route." She looked at Joanna. "You said this paper was the solution to a mystery. What did you mean?"

Joanna took a sip of lemonade. Then she pushed the delicate paper away and settled back in her chair. "Well, it's a kind of crazy story. It all started a little over a year ago, when we were living up in Canada. My husband had just died in an auto accident, and things were pretty tough for me and Josh."

"Go on," Nancy urged gently.

"It seemed as though nothing was working out for us—until we got this phone call from a lawyer in River Heights. He said he'd been working for an elderly woman named Laura Atwood, who'd recently passed away. Well, I didn't know anyone by that name—never even heard of her. So you can imagine how surprised I was when the lawyer told me that Laura Atwood had left everything she owned—her house, her furniture, and the small amount of money in her bank account— to any surviving members of my family. That meant Josh and me!"

"Wow!" Bess exclaimed. "That's really nice. Weird, but nice."

"Anyway, it seemed like the perfect time to move. I needed a change, and here was this beautiful old house ready and waiting for us.

15

We drove to River Heights, saw the place, and decided to move in right away. The money Mrs. Atwood left us was just enough to pay my tuition at college. There wasn't much left over."

"Did you ever find out why Mrs. Atwood left everything to the surviving members of your family?" Nancy wanted to know.

Joanna shook her head. "I asked the lawyer, but he didn't know. He said he was just carrying out her request and that she'd never explained her reasons to him. He was as much in the dark as I was."

"What about the parchment?" asked Nancy. "Where does that fit in?"

"That's the *really* incredible part of the story," Joanna said. "When I met with the lawyer, he told me Laura Atwood's will also mentioned a hidden fortune in gold that she wanted us to have."

"A hidden fortune in gold," Bess repeated dreamily. "That's so romantic!"

Nancy shot an amused glance at her friend. Then she turned back to Joanna. "So you think this parchment might be the key to where the gold is hidden," she said.

Joanna nodded. "There were no clues to the gold's whereabouts in the will," she said. "The lawyer thought that was odd. Laura Atwood wasn't the kind of person who would mention something like that without leaving careful instructions."

Nancy thought for a moment. "Maybe Laura Atwood didn't know about the map," she suggested finally.

"That's possible," Joanna replied. "Anyway," she continued, "the lawyer went through all of Mrs. Atwood's papers, but there wasn't a single clue to the gold's whereabouts. I searched the house and grounds but couldn't find a thing. The gold seemed to have vanished into thin air! You know, I must have looked in that rolltop desk a hundred times, but I was looking for hidden gold, not a secret drawer!"

Bess grinned. "Finding secret drawers is one of Nancy's specialties. She's a terrific detective!"

"Cut it out, Bess," said Nancy in an embarrassed tone.

Joanna smiled at Nancy. "I'm sure Bess is right," she said. Then she added, "To tell you the truth, I'd actually given up on the idea of finding that gold. It all seemed so hopeless that I finally stopped believing it existed at all."

"Until now!" Bess broke in. "This map *proves* the gold exists. And now you've got Nancy to help you follow it straight to your fortune!" She looked at Nancy. "Here's the mystery you've been looking for," she said, grinning.

"It would be incredible if you could find the gold," Joanna said. "Will you take the case?"

Nancy bit her lip thoughtfully. She wanted to take the case, but the map was pretty unclear. She didn't have any idea what the strange drawings could possibly mean or where to start her search.

"Well, I'd love to give it a try," Nancy said slowly. She picked up the map. "But it's not going to be easy. For one thing, these pictures simply don't make sense."

"You'll figure them out eventually," Bess said confidently.

Nancy shook her head. "That's not all," she said, fingering the top edge of the paper. It hadn't looked right to her, and now she knew why. "See how uneven the top of the paper is?" she said to Bess and Joanna. "I'm positive the paper has been torn. We don't even have the whole map."

"Let me see that," Bess said, taking the map from Nancy. She gazed at the top edge. "Nancy, you're right. Look. The sides of the square around the skull continue up to the edge as if they went on past the top of the paper."

"Then I guess we might as well forget the whole thing," Joanna said, shaking her head sadly. "You can't find the gold without the rest of the map." She stared down at the tabletop. After a moment, she raised her head and looked at the girls. "I really shouldn't be so upset," she said with a shrug. "I gave up the idea of ever finding that fortune months ago, so nothing's really different now. It's no big deal."

But Joanna was upset, Nancy could see that. It *was* a big deal. Joanna could really use that money. It would make life a lot easier for her and Josh.

Nancy gave Joanna's hand a squeeze. "We might not have the whole map right now, but I bet we can find the rest of it."

Joanna's expression brightened a little. "Do you really think so?"

"Yes, I do," Nancy replied, trying to sound a lot more confident than she felt. "I'll come back here tomorrow morning and search through the house. If the first part of the map was here, the second half's probably around somewhere, too."

Bess's pretty face spread into a grin. "I'd know that look anywhere. Nancy's already hooked on this mystery, Joanna. I can tell by the do-or-die look in those big blue eyes. You know what? I think you've just gotten yourself a detective."

"Oh, Nancy!" Joanna pulled Nancy to her and gave her a hug. "Thanks for taking the case." Then she turned and hugged Bess. "You two are angels. I can't tell you how much this means to me!"

"Hey," Nancy said, laughing. "Don't thank me until I've solved the mystery!"

Nancy and Bess finished their lemonade and got up to leave. Joanna paid Bess her baby-sitting fee, then walked the girls to the door.

"I'll see you tomorrow morning, Nancy," said Joanna. "Then we can start our search for the rest of the map."

"I'll be here," promised Nancy.

Nancy and Bess said goodbye to Joanna and stepped out of the house into the cool summer night. The fog threaded delicately around them.

"Come on, Bess," Nancy said, hurrying down the porch steps. "I told Dad and Hannah I'd be home half an hour ago. I should have called them, but with all the excitement about the map, I guess I just forgot."

Nancy's mother had died fifteen years before, when Nancy was three. Nancy had been raised by her father, Carson Drew, and the Drews' housekeeper, Hannah Gruen. They trusted Nancy and were used to the late hours she sometimes kept when she was working on a case. But they didn't know about this new case, and Nancy hated to think that they might be worrying about her right now.

"Let's get going," she said to Bess. "Remember, I still have to pick up my car at your house."

Bess nodded. "I've got to get home, too," she said. "But let's *not* take the graveyard shortcut this time, okay?"

"No problem," Nancy said, smiling. "I'm not thrilled about going through Shady Glen Cemetery this late at night, either."

Nancy and Bess walked quickly down the street. When they got to the cemetery, they turned left and headed around the graveyard.

Bess shuddered slightly. "I've lived in this neighborhood all my life, but I don't think I'll *ever* get used to walking past Shady Glen Cemetery on nights like this," she said.

"I know what you mean," Nancy replied. She glanced to the right, through the wrought-iron fence into the foggy graveyard. The tombstones looked like crouching monsters in the swirling mist. The branches of the huge old weeping willow trees hung over the fence like ghostly fingers.

Suddenly both girls froze in their tracks. Bess gasped. The mist had parted for a moment and they'd seen an eerie light moving past the tall pillars of the Mortmain mausoleum.

"Did you see what I saw?" Bess's voice was quivering with terror.

"Take it easy," Nancy said. "The mist is just playing tricks on our eyes. That's probably a white stone statue up there." She broke off as the fog cleared once again.

The ghostly light appeared again at the top of the hill. And a shadowy figure was bathed in its dim glow. The figure seemed to float in midair.

Bess dug her fingernails into Nancy's arm. "Nancy!" she whispered. "That . . . that *thing. It doesn't have any legs!*"

3

At the Curious Cat

The girls stood at the side entrance to the cemetery and stared in horror at the floating figure.

"It's a ghost," squeaked Bess. "What else could it be?"

Nancy studied the figure for a moment. Finally, she realized what they were seeing.

"Bess, it's got to be some normal two-legged person," she stated. "The lower part of his or her body is just hidden by the fog."

A moment later, the mist cleared away completely, revealing a pair of blue jeans beneath a muscular teenage boy's body. The boy was carrying a flashlight.

"I'm glad it's a boy and not a ghost!" Bess said, sighing with relief.

"It's just some kids," Nancy said, watching two more figures appear out of the fog. The light was dim, but Nancy could see that they were both teenage girls. They were wearing jeans and T-shirts. "I wonder if they're the three people we saw before, on our way to Joanna's," she murmured.

"They've seen us, too," Bess said. "They're heading this way."

"Hey," the young man's voice called challengingly. As he came closer, Nancy and Bess could see that he was about Nancy's height—five feet seven—and he had messy sand-colored hair. There was a scowl on his face, and angry brown eyes blinked above high cheekbones.

"Oh no," Bess said with a groan. "It's that creep Ethan Davidson. I never thought I'd see *him* again after graduation."

"Not so loud," Nancy whispered. "He's pretty bad-tempered. Remember all the fights he used to get into?"

"I remember," Bess said in a lower voice. "Nancy, let's get out of here. Ethan's not the greatest person to run into at night near a graveyard." She grabbed Nancy's hand, and the girls started hurrying past the cemetery side gate.

But it was too late. Ethan and his two companions had stepped quickly out of the cemetery and cut them off.

Nancy and Bess recognized the tall, thin,

black-haired teenage girl who was with Ethan. She was Holly Harris, a former classmate of Bess and Nancy. They didn't know the other girl. She was small and slim, with a pretty face and red hair cut very short. She looked to be a few years younger than the other teens.

"Not so fast," Ethan said in a nasty voice. "This party's just beginning." Nancy could see him peering at them through the fog. Then he smiled slowly. "Well, look who's here. Ms. Detective and Bess the teen queen," he said, his voice dripping with contempt.

Nancy and Bess started toward the street, but as they did Ethan, Holly, and the other girl moved closer to them. The threesome formed a tight, menacing circle around the girls. Ethan stood in front of Nancy, his face only inches away from hers. He glared at her with hate-filled eyes.

Nancy met his gaze coolly. Then she forced herself to smile. "Oh, come on, Ethan, give us a break," she said easily. "We're not bothering you, so why don't you just leave us alone?"

Ethan twisted his face into a scowl and leaned toward Nancy. "Because you're too close to our turf," he said, jabbing her shoulder with his finger. "Mine, Holly's, and Kristin's."

"Look," Bess piped up. "We're not on your turf. We're just coming from a baby-sitting job, minding our own business."

Nancy drew her breath in sharply. Somehow, she had the feeling that was the wrong thing to say.

"Baby-sitting," Holly said, sneering. "That figures!"

"You two are real wimps," Kristin put in. Nancy glanced at her. Kristin was chewing a big wad of gum. Her head was cocked to one side and her eyes were half closed as she scowled at them. Suddenly she thrust her face forward, opened her mouth, and began to pop her gum loudly, right near Nancy's ear. Nancy ignored her and turned her gaze back to Ethan.

Ethan narrowed his eyes. "Now, look," he said menacingly to Nancy and Bess. "I want you to listen—*hard*. Stay away from Shady Glen, or else!"

"Or else what?" Nancy asked quietly.

Ethan let out a nasty laugh. "Or some ghost might get you! And if a ghost doesn't get you, maybe my friends and I will!"

It was a threat, and Nancy knew Ethan was the type of guy who carried out his threats.

Nancy took a deep breath. "Okay, Ethan," she said in a calm voice. "We get the message. So why don't you and your friends head back to your turf, and we'll get going."

Nancy continued to look at Ethan coolly. He dropped his eyes and abruptly turned his back on Nancy and Bess. "Let's go," he said to Holly and Kristin. He stepped back into the cemetery, followed closely by Holly and Kristin. A moment later, the three of them had disappeared into the foggy darkness.

"I can't believe that guy," Bess said as she and Nancy hurried down the sidewalk. "You know, I can see Holly hanging out with him. She was always a troublemaker in high school. But I wonder how that other girl, Kristin, got mixed up with him."

"Who knows?" Nancy replied with a shrug. "Anyway," she added, "we won't take this route to Joanna's anymore. No use inviting trouble."

"You can say *that* again," Bess agreed emphatically.

"Joanna, it's just not here," Nancy said wearily, wiping a smudge of dirt from her forehead.

It was late afternoon the next day. Nancy had been searching the Williamses' house since early that morning, from the basement to the attic. She'd checked every piece of furniture Laura Atwood had left the Williamses, felt along every floorboard for a hidden spring that might reveal a second hiding place. She'd come up empty-handed.

Joanna sank into the chair by the rolltop desk and lifted Josh onto her lap. She'd double-checked every place Nancy had looked, and she was tired, too.

"Let's face it," Joanna said. "The other part of that map is gone for good."

Nancy shook her head. "Don't give up hope, Joanna. We may still be able to find the missing piece. And even if we can't, maybe we can trace the gold with the part of the map we have."

Joanna broke into a grin. "Well, if you think we can . . . then I'm sure we will."

Nancy smiled back at her. She liked Joanna, and she didn't want to let her down. She tried to think of other places where the missing half of the map might be. After a moment, her eyes lit up. "Joanna, you said you sold a few pieces of Laura Atwood's furniture. Can you remember which pieces and whom you sold them to?"

"Sure," Joanna said, nodding. "I sold all the stuff to Catherine Hansen. She owns an antique store called the Curious Cat. She said all the furniture was valuable, but she was especially interested in an old wardrobe. It was made out of the same rose-colored wood as this desk. They both have the same design on them, and both were signed by a well-known furniture maker. That's what makes the wardrobe especially valuable."

Nancy nodded, thinking hard. Since the same furniture maker had made both pieces, the wardrobe, like the desk, just might have a secret compartment. It was beginning to look as if the missing part of the map probably *wasn't* out of her reach—as long as Catherine Hansen hadn't already sold the wardrobe.

Nancy got the address of the Curious Cat from Joanna. The store was located in a residential section of River Heights, not too far from the downtown shopping area. Nancy said goodbye to Joanna and Josh and headed outside to her blue sports car. Fifteen minutes later, she was pulling into the driveway of Catherine Hansen's house. It was a freshly painted red and white Victorian-style house on a quiet street. Catherine Hansen had set up shop in her garage, but there were a few beautiful antiques displayed on the lawn. Nancy glanced admiringly at a highly polished dining table and chairs as she made her way across the grass and into the store.

"This place is incredible!" Nancy said as she gazed around the store. Beautifully preserved antiques were crammed into the small garage. Expensive silver candlesticks were arranged decoratively on top of a gleaming glass-topped coffee table. A heavy smoked mirror reflected Nancy's smiling face.

"Glad you like it." Pushing aside her ledger, a short, plump, dark-haired woman who looked to be in her mid-thirties stepped from behind the counter. She smiled warmly and held out her hand. "I'm the owner. Anything in particular I can show you, or are you just browsing?"

Nancy shook Catherine Hansen's hand. "Actually, I'm interested in something a friend of mine sold you a while ago," Nancy told her. "A wardrobe made out of rose-colored wood."

Mrs. Hansen smiled and nodded. "Oh, I remember that wardrobe. I fell in love with it the first time I saw it."

"Do you still have it?" Nancy asked.

Mrs. Hansen motioned to a far corner of the garage. Nancy looked across the room and saw a tall, elegant closet. As Joanna had said, it had been made in the same style as the rolltop desk. Nancy's heart skipped a beat. Hidden in the wardrobe, only a few feet away from her, might be the missing part of the map.

"Do you mind if I look at it more closely?" she asked Mrs. Hansen.

"Help yourself," Mrs. Hansen replied. "But before you do, would you mind signing my guest book?" She indicated an open notebook lying on an antique book stand by the door. "I like to inform customers of any special sales I might be having in the future."

Nancy obligingly stepped over to the book and wrote down her name and address. Mrs. Hansen thanked her. Then she headed back to the counter and began to leaf through her ledger again.

Nancy threaded her way through a maze of dressers and tables over to the wardrobe. She knelt down and edged the door open. There was a single six-inch-deep drawer in the bottom of the closet. Nancy pulled open the drawer and immediately noticed that it was shallower inside by two inches—just like the bottom drawer in the rolltop desk.

Just then, Nancy heard someone walk into the store. "Hey, Mom," came a teenage girl's voice. "Are you coming in for dinner?"

"In a minute, honey," Mrs. Hansen replied absently.

Somehow, the girl's voice sounded familiar to Nancy, but she couldn't remember where she'd heard it. Nancy turned to see if she could recognize the girl, but she had left the shop. Nancy turned her attention back to the drawer. She reached slowly into the back of it. The wood felt smooth to her touch. She ran her fingers along the inside of the drawer. A second later, her thumb hit a pit in the wood. She slipped her nail underneath it and pulled. Instantly, the wood plank flipped up, revealing a secret compartment. Nancy stared at the hidden pocket in the drawer in disbelief.

The hidden compartment was empty except for a tattered blue ribbon.

Nancy grasped the ribbon curiously. It was the same type that had been tied around the map part she'd found in Joanna's desk. So the other piece of the map *had* been here. But why wasn't it here now?

Nancy shook her head, frustration washing over her. The only answer was that someone else had found the secret drawer—and the missing part of the map. But who? And had that someone found the missing map part before Joanna sold the wardrobe or afterward?

Nancy sighed. Without the missing part of the map, the gold was going to be a lot harder to find.

Nancy dropped the ribbon back into the hidden compartment and pushed the drawer back into place. Then she stood up, brushing the dust off her jeans.

As she stepped to the front of the store, Mrs. Hansen looked up at her and smiled. "Do you like the wardrobe?" the antique dealer asked.

"It's beautiful," Nancy replied. "Thanks for letting me look at it so closely."

"No problem," Mrs. Hansen said pleasantly.

Could *she* have been the one who'd found the missing piece of the map? Nancy wondered. It was a good possibility. And if she hadn't found it, maybe she knew who had.

"Actually," Nancy said, "maybe you can help me. Did anyone else come in here and look at that wardrobe?"

Mrs. Hansen shook her head. "It's been in my workshop for months. I had to do some work on it—refinishing the wood and polishing it. I only just got it into the shop this afternoon. You're the first customer to see it."

Nancy nodded. Then she took a deep breath. "Mrs. Hansen, did you find anything inside the wardrobe?"

Mrs. Hansen raised her eyebrows. "No, I didn't," she said. "Why? Did your friend lose something?"

"Um, you could say that," Nancy replied. "Did you notice anything unusual about the wardrobe when you were working on it?"

Mrs. Hansen shrugged. "Can't say I did."

Nancy watched the other woman's face as she responded. There was no change of expression or hesitation—nothing to suggest she wasn't telling the truth.

"Well, thanks, Mrs. Hansen," Nancy told the store owner pleasantly. "You've really helped me."

"No problem. And good luck. I hope your friend finds what she's looking for," she answered.

Nancy hurried out the door and across the lawn to her car. She kept thinking about the missing half of the map. If Mrs. Hansen didn't have it, then who did? And did that person know how valuable it was?

Nancy stepped to her car. "Uh-oh," she said, groaning. A carefully folded piece of paper had been stuck underneath her windshield wiper blade. "This can't be a ticket," she said to herself. "I mean, there's nothing illegal about parking in a driveway." Nancy pulled the note free and opened it. She gasped as she read the hastily scribbled message.

"Curiosity killed the cat. What about Nancy Drew?"

4

Break-in at Bess's House

Nancy's face was grim as she reread the short threatening message. She was pretty sure that the writer of the note was the same person who had found the missing part of the map. He or she must have known or guessed that the map led to something valuable. What else could the note be but a warning to Nancy to drop her search?

Nancy looked at the shop. Catherine Hansen had told her she hadn't found anything inside the wardrobe. Now Nancy was beginning to wonder if the antique dealer had been lying. She might have taken the map apart, then gotten nervous when she saw Nancy inspecting the wardrobe. She could easily have written the note, slipped outside, and placed it on the car while Nancy was examining the wardrobe.

Nancy thought about going back inside the

Curious Cat to confront Catherine Hansen, but she was positive the woman would claim she hadn't found the map or written the note. And even though the note seemed to point to Mrs. Hansen, Nancy couldn't be absolutely sure the antiques dealer had found the map or written the note.

But Nancy was sure of one thing. Someone else—possibly Catherine Hansen—was searching for the gold. Nancy took a deep breath. Now she'd need to move really fast and work extra carefully. Since the map piece was clearly gone for good, she'd just have to do her best with the part she did have. She just hoped she could find the gold before her rival tracked his or her way to it.

Nancy got into her car, started the engine, and headed down the street toward home. The evening sky gleamed with the pink light of the setting sun. A few minutes later, Nancy pulled into her driveway.

"Dad? Hannah?" she called as she walked into the house.

"Nancy? We're in here," Carson Drew called back from the kitchen.

When Nancy got to the kitchen, she found her father munching on a roast beef sandwich and watching the evening news on TV. Hannah, a gray-haired middle-aged woman, was standing at the counter frosting a chocolate cake. Nancy gave her a hug. Then she stepped over to her father. "Hi, Dad," she said, dropping a kiss onto his cheek. "How's your current case coming?" Nancy's father was a distinguished lawyer.

"It's going pretty well," Carson told his daughter. "I'm just taking a little dinner break from my work. I didn't realize you'd be home or I would have waited to have dinner with you. By the way, it looks as if I'm going to have to go out of town later this week."

"Nancy and I will be just fine on our own, won't we?" Hannah said, smiling at Nancy. She placed more roast beef and bread on the table.

Nancy sat down and began to make a sandwich. "Right, Dad. But we'll miss you!"

Carson Drew gave his daughter an affectionate look.

"What's up?" he asked her. "You looked pretty excited this morning. New case?"

"Brand-new. And this one is *really* incredible."

"Oh, you say that about all your cases," Mr. Drew said teasingly.

Nancy smiled and nodded. "I know I do—but that's because all of them really are incredible."

"Oh, I almost forgot. Bess has been calling here all afternoon," Hannah said, shaking her head. "It was getting so hard for your father to work that he finally had to turn on the answering machine."

Nancy laughed. "It was probably something desperate—like what to wear Friday night for her date. I'll call her back later. Right now, I need to eat dinner and then get to work."

After dinner, Carson disappeared into his study and Nancy spread the map out on the kitchen table and began to study it.

There were the strange, crudely drawn pictures again, laid out before her like a top-secret code—the rooster, the fire-breathing dragon, and the skull inside the box.

Nancy tried to concentrate on the map, but the TV news program kept intruding into her thoughts. "On the local side," she heard the announcer say, "there have been a number of robberies in River Heights recently. Police detectives say the break-ins have a similar pattern to a few that occurred over a year ago. A husband and wife team, Jim and Francesca Rollins, were convicted for those earlier burglaries."

Nancy glanced up at the TV. On the screen was a file photo of a couple who looked to be in their late twenties. Francesca Rollins had short brown hair and was wearing a denim jumpsuit. Her husband, Jim, had blond hair and a muscular build.

The newscaster continued. "The Rollinses were released from prison three weeks ago and are now being sought for questioning. So far, the police have not been able to find them."

There was a slight pause. Then the newscaster said, "And now for a look at the weather. Well, Big Bob, what's in store for us tomorrow?"

Nancy got up and switched off the TV. Then she sat back down at the table. Leaning on her elbows, she glued her eyes to the yellowed map and thought—hard.

It was clear to her that the stiff, awkward drawings were symbols—symbols for things or places. But *which* places? They could be anywhere.

It was likely that the places were somewhere in or close to River Heights, Nancy reasoned, since Laura Atwood had lived in town and would probably have hidden her gold near her house. But River Heights was a fairly big place, and the suburbs surrounding it stretched on for miles.

Nancy studied the map closely, but after an hour, it still didn't make sense to her. She shook her head. "This is really hopeless," she said with a sigh.

Suddenly the quiet of the evening was shattered by the ring of the telephone.

"I'll get it," Nancy called. She jumped up and headed across the kitchen to the wall phone by the door. "Hello?" she said into the receiver.

"Nancy?" she heard Bess's voice say. "Thank goodness you're home. I've been trying to get you all day." Bess's voice was shaking. She sounded close to tears.

"I've been out investigating Joanna's case. Bess, what's wrong? You sound really upset."

"I *am* upset. Nancy, our house was broken into today!"

"You're kidding!" Nancy exclaimed.

"No, I'm not," Bess told her. "We were robbed—completely cleaned out!"

"Oh, Bess! That's terrible!" Nancy said.

"They took our TV, stereo, VCR, and silverware. They even took some of my jewelry."

"You weren't in the house when it happened, were you?" Nancy asked in an alarmed voice.

"No, I was out shopping, and my parents were at work," Bess said. "Anyway," she continued, "the police were here. They said the break-in fits the pattern of the other thefts around here—and the ones the Rollinses pulled before they were caught and sent to jail. The police are convinced the Rollinses are responsible. Nancy, it's so scary. The whole area's being terrorized by those people."

"When did the robbery take place?" Nancy wanted to know.

She could hear Bess take a deep breath. Then her friend said, "Well, according to the police, our burglar alarm went off at about eleven-thirty this morning. A police car was only a few blocks from our house, but when it got here, the thieves were gone!"

"Wow!" Nancy exclaimed into the phone. "The thieves really worked fast!"

"The police say it's just good planning—and they've probably been staking out the house."

Bess paused for a moment. Nancy had a feeling she knew what her friend was going to say next.

"Uh, Nancy?" Bess said, tentatively.

Nancy sighed. "Okay, Bess. I know what you're going to ask me."

"Well, it *would* be great if you could investigate this."

Nancy bit her lip. Tracking the Rollinses was going to take her away from Joanna's case. But how could she refuse to help her best friend? She wanted to get the Marvins' stuff back. And, more important, if she caught the Rollinses, she'd put an end to the robberies that had plagued Bess's—and Joanna's—neighborhood.

"Okay, Bess," Nancy said. "I'll be over in half an hour to see if I can dig up any leads."

"Great!" Bess said excitedly. "I knew I could count on you!"

"Look, don't get your hopes up too high. If the police haven't been able to track down the Rollinses, there's no reason to think *I* can."

* * *

A little while later, Nancy was kneeling on the lawn in front of the Marvins' house. She aimed her flashlight at the brown-streaked tire tracks that cut across the grass. Clearly, the burglars had driven right up to the house for a faster getaway. From the thick width of the tire prints, Nancy guessed that they'd probably used a pickup truck or a van.

Nancy looked up at Bess. "What did the police say about these tracks?" she asked.

"That they're a trademark of robberies pulled by Jim and Francesca Rollins. They used a pickup truck for all those other robberies they carried out over a year ago. It's just one of the things that make the police sure those two are responsible."

"Is that all they said?" Nancy asked.

"That's it," replied Bess.

"Well, I'll tell you what these tracks tell me." Nancy glanced toward the woods at the end of Bess's street. "Those crooks headed into the woods. They didn't drive back into town after they burglarized your house."

Bess stared at Nancy with a puzzled expression. "How do you know that?" she asked.

"Because the tracks *come* from town. If the thieves had made a U-turn in order to drive back there, we'd see the tire tracks in the grass. But instead, the tracks go in the other direction, *away* from town." Nancy shone her flashlight onto the pavement. "See?" she said. "The tracks continue into the street and head toward the woods."

Bess nodded as she peered at the pavement. "That's amazing," she said. "I don't think the police figured that out." She looked at Nancy. "Do you think the Rollinses are hiding out in the woods?" she asked.

"It's a possibility," Nancy replied, nodding. "Another possibility is that they've stashed the stolen goods there. A house or cabin in the forest would be a perfect hiding place. The police may not have thought of looking there."

"But how would we follow the tracks to the hideout?" Bess asked. "They stop just past the paved part of the road."

"Chances are the Rollinses drove down one of the dirt roads into the woods. I'll just have to find the right road and match up the tire tracks."

Bess sucked in her breath. "Well, what are we waiting for? Let's get going."

Nancy blinked at her friend in disbelief. "Bess, you're not actually *volunteering* to go with me, are you? Into the woods? At night?"

Bess tossed her head. "Why not? It's my family's stuff. I should help find it. You know, I'm not *quite* as chicken as you think."

Nancy smothered a grin. She'd make sure to remind Bess how brave she was the next time she refused to get involved in an investigation that seemed too dangerous.

Nancy looked up at the sky. There was no moon. In the dark, even with a flashlight, it could take them hours to find the right road.

"Actually," Nancy said, "I think this search had better wait until tomorrow morning. It'll be really difficult in the dark. Even if we locate the hideout tonight, I'd hate to find the Rollinses there, dumping the stuff from another robbery."

A horrified expression flashed across Bess's face. Nancy realized that her friend hadn't thought of the possibility of meeting up with the thieves when she'd offered to help. But in spite of her fear, Bess was determined to help Nancy track down the Rollinses. "We'll just have to start searching tomorrow," she said cheerfully.

Nancy smiled at her. Then she said, "I almost forgot—I've got an update for you on the gold investigation." She filled her friend in on her visit to the Curious Cat, finding the blue ribbon in the empty drawer, discovering the note on her car, and her suspicions about Catherine Hansen.

When she had finished, Bess said anxiously, "Nancy, it would be awful if someone else found Joanna's gold."

Nancy nodded. The possibility that someone else might find the gold first was worrying her, too, but she couldn't think about that now. She had promised Bess she'd investigate the robbery. The search for the gold would have to wait.

Nancy arrived at Bess's house early the next morning. They began their search at the end of Bess's street, where a dirt road led into the woods.

By late morning, they'd checked out five of the roads leading into the forest. They'd followed each road for at least a mile on foot. But they hadn't found any tire tracks.

"This is the last one," Nancy said as she braked her car to a stop next to another dirt road.

"Let's hope it's *the* one," Bess said as they got out of the car. "I'm starting to get a crick in my neck from staring at the ground."

They followed the road, their heads down, searching for the tracks. After they had walked for about a half-mile, they straightened up. Bess began to massage her neck. Nancy held her hand to her forehead to shield her eyes from the sun. She peered down the road.

Suddenly she saw them. The tracks were on the other side of a small mud puddle. Nancy raced over to the tracks and knelt down beside them.

"I've found them!" she cried.

Bess hurried over to her. "Are you sure?" she asked.

Nancy nodded emphatically. "I'm sure. See

the double-V pattern and the wide tread? These tracks are exactly like the ones on your lawn!"

Nancy stood up, and she and Bess began to follow the tracks down the road.

"I just thought of something," Bess said suddenly. "If the Rollinses drove down this dirt road, how come we didn't see any tire tracks before now?"

"Maybe they started to cover up the tracks, then decided they didn't need to keep doing it," Nancy replied. "They probably figured the police would stop looking past a certain point."

"I don't know," Bess said, shaking her head. "If I were a professional thief, I'd make sure I covered *all* my tracks."

"Bess Marvin, hardened criminal," Nancy said jokingly.

Bess made a face at her. "Well, if you ask me, this is a pretty amateur way to make a getaway," she stated.

The girls continued down the road. Then, just around a hairpin curve, they spotted a tiny abandoned cabin, half hidden in the thick brush.

"Wow, that place looks ancient," Bess said.

"Look," Nancy said, pointing at the ground. "The tire tracks stop right here."

"*Somebody's* been here," Bess said. She pointed to a few empty soft drink cans and

46

crumpled candy wrappers lying on the ground.
"What slobs!" she added in a disgusted voice.

"Come on, let's check out that cabin," Nancy said.

"What if the Rollinses are inside right now?" Bess asked, her voice suddenly very soft. "I mean, it's probably not safe."

"There's no truck around here, so it's a good bet that the Rollinses are gone for the moment," replied Nancy.

She started to work her way through the brush to the cabin.

"I hope you're right," Bess said with a sigh as she followed her friend.

When they reached the cabin, they saw that all the windows were masked by brand-new metal plates. Nancy stepped up to the door. It was fastened with a padlock that also looked brand-new.

"Someone's taken a lot of trouble to make sure no one can get in here," Nancy commented.

"Well, how do *we* get in?" Bess wanted to know.

"I could pick the lock. But that would take a while—and I don't think we should stick around long enough for the Rollinses to come back and find us." Nancy bit her lip thoughtfully. "Maybe there's another way in," she said finally.

Nancy circled the little building. As she walked, she noticed that the old boards of the walls weren't fastened very solidly. She found a board that seemed to fit more loosely than the others and began to pull with all her strength. "Bess, I need your help!" she called. Bess hurried over to Nancy and grabbed the lower part of the board.

The girls tugged and pulled. Finally, they heard a creaking sound. The rusty nails were easing out of the wood. A moment later, they pulled the board free.

"Whew," said Bess, wiping the perspiration off her forehead. "What a job!"

"I'm going in," Nancy said. She eased through the gap in the wall, taking care not to scrape her skin on the rusty nails that stuck out dangerously on all sides.

The gap in the wall allowed some light to filter into the cabin. Nancy gave her eyes a moment to adjust to the dimness. Soon she was able to make out the contents of the room.

There was an old chair, a broken table standing against a wall, and nothing else.

Nancy couldn't believe it. The place was almost totally bare. Had she and Bess tracked their way to a dead end?

5

The Trail of the Treasure Map

"Nancy! What's in there?" Bess's voice called from outside.

Nancy sighed in frustration as she walked back to the gap in the wall. "Nothing's in here," she responded.

Bess sighed, then stepped carefully inside the cabin. She shook her head in disbelief when she saw the single chair and broken table. "It doesn't make sense," she said. "Those tire tracks matched up perfectly!"

"I know they did," replied Nancy. "Maybe they belonged to a completely different truck, after all. Anyway, there goes our only clue. Now we'll never find the stolen stuff or the Rollinses. I'm sorry, Bess."

Nancy looked at her friend. Bess was staring down at the floor, a disappointed expression on her face. After a moment she raised her head

49

and gave Nancy a weak smile. "That's okay," Bess said. "You did your best."

But Nancy was angry with herself. Bess had counted on her, and she'd let her down. She looked around the cabin one more time, to be absolutely certain she hadn't missed any clues.

"I'm going back outside," Bess said. "The air is so stale in here."

Nancy nodded absently as she gazed around the room. Suddenly she spotted something on the wall above the broken table. Nancy stepped across the cabin and peered at the wall. Someone had drawn a lumpy, shapeless tree on it in bright red paint.

Nancy wondered if the drawing had been freshly painted. She leaned across the table and ran her hand over the drawing. The paint felt smooth and dry to her touch. There was no sign that the paint had peeled. If the drawing had been on the wall for a long time, the paint would have peeled in places by now, and the color would have faded. Nancy leaned a little closer to the wall. As she did, her body touched the rickety old table. The table swayed once, then crashed to the floor.

Nancy frowned. There was something odd about the sound of that table hitting the floor. She knelt down next to the fallen table and rapped on the floor with her knuckles. Instantly, she realized what that strange sound meant.

There was a hollow space under the floorboards.

Just then she heard Bess come back into the cabin. "I thought we were leaving," Bess was saying impatiently. Her eyes widened when she saw Nancy kneeling on the floor. "What on earth are you doing?" Bess asked.

"Looking for a trapdoor," replied Nancy. She felt around the floor with both hands. After a moment, her right hand touched a large knothole. Nancy slipped her hand under the wedge at one end of the knothole and pulled. A square section of the floor moved. It *was* a trapdoor! Nancy pulled harder, and the trapdoor opened.

Nancy stared into the space below the floorboards. "Bess, look at this!" she said excitedly. "There's a secret room down here!"

She reached into her purse for her small flashlight, clicked it on, and shone it into the room. "It doesn't look very deep," she reported. She turned off the flashlight and stuck it in the pocket of her shorts. Then she squeezed herself through the small trapdoor. A moment later, her feet made contact with the room's dirt floor.

"If you think I'm staying up here in this creepy shack by myself, you're crazy," she heard Bess say. "I'm coming down, too!"

Nancy pulled out the flashlight and trained

the beam on her friend to help light her way. Seconds later, Bess was standing beside her. Eagerly Nancy shone the flashlight around the room, but it was soon obvious to both girls that this room was empty, too.

"Another dead end," Bess said with a groan.

"It sure looks that way," Nancy replied grimly. She thought for a minute. Then she shook her head. "I just can't believe someone would dig a secret room like this without a reason," she said. "This *has* to be the place where the Rollinses stash the stolen goods."

"Well, then, where's the stuff, then?" Bess said, looking around the empty room.

"They must have moved it to another hideout," replied Nancy. "Or maybe they gave the stuff to a fence—someone who would resell the stolen goods for them."

Nancy aimed the light around the room again. She should have known the Rollinses would be too professional to leave anything behind that would incriminate them.

Suddenly a tiny flash in the far corner caught her eye. She hurried over to it. Something round and gold-colored lay in the damp dirt. She reached down and picked up the small object. On closer inspection she saw that it was a gold earring engraved with a flower.

"What is it?" Bess asked curiously.

Nancy held the earring out to Bess. "It just

might be the evidence we've been looking for," she replied, grinning.

"Hey, that's my earring!" Bess exclaimed.

Nancy handed her the earring. "Are you sure it's yours?" she asked carefully.

Bess nodded emphatically. "Of course I'm sure," she said firmly. "It's from my favorite pair. I wore them on my last date. Those earrings were a Sweet Sixteen present from my parents. They were stolen yesterday, along with my other jewelry."

"Then that proves the thieves were here," Nancy said. "And they'll probably use this room again as a hiding place."

"Let's get out of here," Bess said with a shudder. "For all we know, the Rollinses might be on their way to this cabin right now!"

After they had climbed back up into the cabin, Nancy carefully closed the trapdoor and picked up the table. Then she took one last look at the tree drawing on the wall.

"We were lucky," she said with a smile. "If I hadn't come over here to look at this drawing and knocked over the table, we never would have found the secret room or your earring."

"Let's make sure we stay lucky," Bess countered. "Let's leave before the thieves come back. Besides, I'm supposed to baby-sit for Josh again tonight, and I want to take a nice long shower first." She ran her fingers through her dirty hair. "Yuck! I feel like the inside of a vacuum cleaner!"

When they left the cabin, Nancy carefully placed the board over the gap in the wall so that the thieves wouldn't know anyone had been there. Then the girls hurried down the road to Nancy's car. Nancy drove Bess home. Then she headed back to her own house, following a route that took her past Shady Glen Cemetery and Joanna's house.

Nancy was glad she'd made some progress on the robbery case. She only wished she'd gotten as far with the search for Joanna's gold. That map still had her stumped. She sighed as she turned into Joanna's street. Somehow she had to figure out what those pictures meant and where those straight lines led to. And somewhere out there was a person—maybe Catherine Hansen—who had the missing half of the map and might be hot on the gold's trail this very moment!

Nancy slowed down as Joanna's stately home came into view. She stopped her car in front of the house. Potted plants stood on the huge old porch, their leaves fluttering peacefully in the breeze. On the roof, a rooster-shaped weather vane turned slightly as the wind changed direction. Nancy saw that the weather vane exactly matched the rooster knocker on Joanna's front door. Whoever had the house built must have really liked roosters, Nancy thought.

Suddenly Nancy remembered the rooster drawing on the map. All at once, she realized that whoever had hidden the gold and drawn the map had used the rooster as a symbol of the house. Did that mean the gold was hidden there after all?

One thing Nancy did know for sure now: if the gold wasn't in the house, it had to be hidden somewhere in the neighborhood. But where? Nancy began to go over the map with her mind's eye. Now that she'd figured out the meaning of the rooster symbol, maybe she'd be able to make sense of the other drawings.

First she pictured the dark lines that ran from the rooster to the large square with the skull inside it. What could the skull possibly symbolize?

Then it hit her. The skull could stand for a cemetery. And Joanna's house was just a few blocks from Shady Glen! It was just possible that the square marked the fence which surrounded the graveyard.

So far, so good, thought Nancy. Now there was just one more drawing to decipher: the fire-breathing dragon. Nancy concentrated hard, trying to picture the drawing's placement on the map. She was pretty sure the dragon drawing came after a few dark lines that ran past the cemetery. There were several houses over that way—most of them large mansions built over a hundred years ago.

Nancy put her sports car into drive and headed toward Oakwood Avenue, where most of the mansions stood. Soon she passed the cemetery. She turned right into Oakwood Avenue and began to cruise slowly down the wide, oak-lined street. She studied the front of each mansion carefully. None of them featured a dragon as part of its design.

"Okay, let's try the side streets," Nancy murmured to herself. She turned her car down Rutledge Lane, a dead-end street. There was Daniel Mortmain's old mansion. The house had been abandoned for years. When Nancy was younger, she and her friends had decided it was haunted. They'd taken turns daring each other to run up the decaying front steps and ring the rusty old bell. No one had ever had the courage to sneak inside the house, though.

Looking at the boarded-up old house now, Nancy wondered why no one had bought it in recent years and restored it. It was a beautiful place and different from all the other houses in the neighborhood. It had been built in a southern style, with huge white columns and a wide front porch.

Nancy eased to a stop in front of the house and studied it with a smile. She and her friends used to imagine that there were ghosts hiding behind those columns, just waiting to spring out at them. She let her gaze travel up to the top of the columns.

Suddenly Nancy gulped in amazement. At the top of each column, just below the roof, was a dragon. The dragons had been sculpted into the wood, and they were breathing fire!

"That's it!" Nancy shouted, giving the sports car's horn a tiny, triumphant toot. She'd cracked the map's code!

But knowing which spots were marked on the map was only the beginning. She hadn't yet found the gold. She still had a lot of searching to do.

The gold might be hidden somewhere in Joanna's house, Nancy realized. Or it could be hidden in the Mortmain mansion. She turned off the ignition and got out of the car.

The broken-down front steps were exactly as Nancy remembered them, and the doors were still nailed tightly shut. But as Nancy walked down the wide porch, she noticed that a board covering one of the large doorlike ground-floor windows seemed loose. Nancy pulled at the board and, to her surprise, it gave instantly. She slipped between the board and the window, took hold of the clasp, and pushed.

The window opened easily. A moment later, Nancy was standing inside the Mortmain mansion.

Nancy gazed around the musty old mansion. The room she was standing in looked like an entrance hall. A cobweb-covered chandelier hovered above sheet-draped furniture. There was dust everywhere—on the banister, on the windowsills, and all over the floor.

Nancy suddenly noticed that a wide dust-free path ran across the middle of the floor. It looked as if something—or someone—had been dragged across the floor.

Nancy shivered slightly. Stop it! she told herself. You've been watching too many dumb horror movies!

What could have made that path? The other person who was looking for the gold? How could that person have known that the Mortmain mansion was important in the search unless the drawing of the dragon was on that person's part of the map, too? Nancy thought for a minute, then shook her head. It didn't seem likely that the dragon drawing would have been repeated. There was no way her rival could have found out about the Mortmain mansion.

There had to be a perfectly logical explanation for the path, Nancy told herself.

She took a deep breath and started down the hallway. Keeping her gaze on the dust-free path, she followed it to a large windowless room. The door to the room was wide open.

Nancy stepped inside the room and looked around. The only piece of furniture in the room was a tall empty bookcase standing against one wall. There was another door on the other side of the room. It stood partway open.

Nancy walked over to the doorway and peered through it. On the other side of the door were wooden steps leading down to what appeared to be the cellar. She looked down at the floor. The dust-free path stopped right at this door.

Just then, Nancy heard a car squeal to a stop right in front of the mansion. Then there was the sound of a car door slamming. Nancy ran back to the door that led to the hall and listened hard for the sounds of someone entering the mansion. She didn't hear the loosely hinged cellar door close with a soft click.

For a moment, she heard nothing. Then her ears picked up the sound of footsteps against the wooden floor. The footsteps became louder, echoing through the house.

Nancy closed the hall door quickly but quietly. Then she hurried back to the cellar door and turned the knob. The door was now locked! She looked around for a place to hide. But the only piece of furniture in the room was the huge bookcase.

Nancy's throat went dry as she realized she was trapped! There was nowhere to hide.

And the footsteps were right outside the room.

6

Nancy on Top of the Case

Nancy had to think fast. In another moment, she'd be discovered. There had to be somewhere to hide, she thought as she stared around the empty room. But all she saw was a locked door and the old bookcase. There wasn't a hiding place in sight. Unless . . .

Nancy looked at the bookcase. It didn't quite reach the ceiling, and there seemed to be just enough space between the top and the ceiling for a person to lie flat. She could use the shelves of the bookcase as a ladder. No one would see her up there.

Nancy hurried over to the bookcase and grabbed one of the upper shelves. She took a deep breath and stepped up onto one of the lower shelves, hoping desperately that the bookcase was sturdy enough to hold her and that it wouldn't topple over.

The bookcase remained steady. Nancy let out a sigh of relief and continued to climb. When she got to the top, she lifted herself up over the edge. Then she slid along the top on her stomach. She had reached the top just in time. She heard the door to the room open and a girl's hushed voice say, "She's got to be in here."

Then a boy's voice said, "Well, I don't see her, do you?"

Then Nancy heard a second girl's voice say nastily, "I know it's that pain, Nancy Drew, again. I recognized her car."

"So did I," said the other girl. "It's sooo ugly!"

The voices were muffled, and Nancy didn't recognize them, but it was clear from their conversation that they were looking for her. Her car, parked outside in plain view, had given her away.

Nancy was sure that their original purpose in coming to the mansion was to search for the gold. They had the missing part of the map. The mansion must have been marked on their part, too.

It was very hot up there, and the top of the bookcase was covered with dust. Nancy's nose began to tingle, signaling the start of a sneeze. She covered her nose with her hand. The tingling stopped.

Nancy couldn't stand it any longer. She

61

had to see who was down there in the room.

Noiselessly, she slid to the edge of the bookcase and peered over the side. She stared down at the trio below her in disbelief. It was Ethan Davidson, Holly Harris, and their friend Kristin.

Nancy couldn't believe her eyes. How could those three be involved in the search for the hidden gold? It just didn't make sense. Ethan and Holly didn't seem like the type who would take the time to figure out an old treasure map. They'd lose interest right away. The only thing all three of them seemed to be interested in was acting tough.

The three of them left the room. Nancy decided to stay in her hiding place for a few minutes in case they came back.

As she lay there, she remembered all she knew about Ethan and Holly. Ethan had always been a bully, ever since elementary school days.

Holly had been suspended from high school twice for cheating. She'd also been caught shoplifting in a downtown department store.

Kristin was still a bit of a mystery to Nancy. She wondered how the younger teen had gotten involved with Ethan and Holly.

If those three were looking for the gold, it did explain why Ethan had been so threatening in the cemetery the other night. Maybe the gold was hidden there. It would make sense that the trio would try to protect the area from intruders.

But if the gold was in the cemetery, what were they doing at the Mortmain house? And she still couldn't believe that the three of them would enjoy tracking down hidden gold.

Something else puzzled Nancy. It made sense that Holly would be able to spot her car—she and Nancy had known each other casually for years. But how did Kristin know what her car looked like? She'd said she recognized it, but Nancy had barely been aware of her existence until two days ago.

Just then, the trio came back into the room. "How could that little snitch have slipped past us?" Holly said angrily.

"Do you think she's hiding upstairs?" Kristin asked.

Nancy laughed to herself. They'd never guess she was right over them, listening to every word they were saying.

"She must be on to us," Ethan replied thoughtfully.

"Well, if she ruins this setup for us, she'll be really sorry!"

"Don't worry, Holly." Ethan's voice was reassuring. "I've planned a little surprise for our nosy Nancy. We'll stake out her car. Then, when she comes out, we'll make sure she stays out of our business—permanently!" He laughed

63

menacingly, and Nancy could hear the two girls join in. "Come on," Ethan continued. "I've got the perfect idea for a new setup. . . ."

The three teens left the room. Nancy glared after them angrily. So they were planning to gang up on her, three against one. Well, let them try, Nancy thought. After all, she knew what they were up to. And she'd fight back if she had to.

Nancy preferred to avoid a confrontation. She was pretty certain that if she tried to take all three of them on at once, she'd wind up wishing she hadn't. But how was she going to get to her car without them seeing her?

Sighing, she realized that she couldn't. She'd have to sneak out the back way. She hoped there was another loose board on a back window or door of the Mortmain mansion.

Nancy nodded. Avoiding that trio of bullies was definitely the smart thing to do.

She knew it was a long walk home, and since her father was away on business, she couldn't call him from a pay phone to come pick her up. Hannah was visiting a sick friend, so Nancy was out of luck there too. She'd have to walk.

Nancy slid toward the end of the bookcase and eased her legs down onto one of the upper shelves. Holding on tightly, she began to climb back down to the floor.

When Nancy reached the floor, she stood still for a moment, her forehead pressed against the cool wood of the bookcase. Then she turned and headed for the door.

After she left the room, Nancy headed down a hallway to the back of the mansion.

Maybe Bess would be able to give her a ride home, Nancy thought as she walked. Then she remembered that Bess was baby-sitting for Josh again tonight. Nancy decided to head for Joanna's home, which wasn't too far away. She would tell Bess what had happened; then, later, she'd come back here and pick up her car.

After walking past a number of rooms, Nancy finally reached the back door. To her surprise, it was uncovered and unlocked. She opened it and slipped outside into the warmth of the afternoon, leaving Ethan, Holly, and Kristin far behind.

"So, stop slurping, and tell me what happened!" Bess said impatiently.

Nancy and Bess were sitting in Joanna's kitchen. Bess had made them both root-beer floats. Nancy had been so thirsty she'd downed her float in five minutes.

Nancy stuck her straw into the empty glass and pushed the glass aside. Then she told her friend how she'd figured out the drawings on the map. Bess's eyes grew wide with amazement as Nancy related the series of events that had taken place at the Mortmain mansion.

"That's the story," she said to Bess when she had finished.

"What about Catherine Hansen?" asked Bess. "Is she still a suspect?"

Nancy thought for a minute. Then she shook her head. "No," she said. "I can't see her teaming up with Ethan, Holly, and Kristin to search for gold. Anyway, those three seem pretty tight to me. I doubt if they'd want another partner in on the search."

"Well, I don't know where we go from here," Bess said, "but then, solving mysteries was never my strong point. Anyway," she continued, fingering the gold earring she and Nancy had found that afternoon, "if you could find the mate to this earring, I think I'd just faint with relief. Nancy, they were my favorites!"

Nancy laughed. "I know, Bess, I know. You keep telling me that!"

Bess made a face at her. Then, slowly, the corners of her mouth began turning up, and she started to giggle. "Can you believe it?" she said with a laugh. "I think I actually love these earrings more than . . . more than . . ."

"More than root-beer floats?" Nancy said teasingly.

"Definitely!" Bess said, laughing harder.

"More than—" Nancy broke off in midsentence. She thought she'd heard a faint sound somewhere in the house. "Bess, did you hear

66

something?'' she asked anxiously. "A grinding sound?''

Bess listened for a moment. Then she shook her head.

"No, you must be imagin—" Bess broke off, too, as a loud scraping noise filled the room. "It—it's coming from the basement," she whispered fearfully.

Just then a series of scraping sounds echoed through the house.

Nancy stood up and started for the basement door.

"Wh-where are you going?" Bess asked, her voice catching in her throat.

"Someone is creeping around in Joanna's basement!" Nancy said. "And I'm going to find out who it is!"

7

The Thieves Strike Again

"You're not going down there!" Bess exclaimed in a horrified voice.

"I have to," Nancy replied firmly.

"But what if it's the Rollinses? They're pros, Nancy. They could hurt you!"

Nancy pressed her lips together in determination. Then she marched out of the kitchen to the hall closet. She rummaged around in the closet until she found Josh Williams's baseball bat. She hoped she wouldn't need it, but she knew she'd feel a lot safer having it on hand. She gripped the bat tightly, then hurried to the cellar door and pulled it open.

The noises were much louder now, and there were banging sounds, too. Nancy could also hear muffled voices.

"Wait!" Bess whispered behind her. "I-I'm coming, too."

Nancy smiled at her. The girls started feeling their way slowly down the steep cellar steps in the dark. Nancy didn't want to turn on any lights and alert whoever was downstairs until she had to.

"Do you think it's the thieves?" Bess asked softly as they crept down the stairs. "I don't see how they would have gotten in without us hearing them."

"What I want to know," Nancy whispered back, "is why they would have started in the basement, where the valuable stuff most definitely *wouldn't* be stored? It doesn't fit the pattern of these robberies. The thieves never hit a house when people are home."

"Maybe they just messed up this time," Bess suggested.

"Maybe," Nancy replied. The banging sounds in the basement made her head throb. She gripped Josh's bat a little more tightly.

Three more steps . . . two more . . . Nancy reached for the light switch at the bottom of the stairs and flicked it on. Instantly the basement was flooded with light.

The girls blinked at the sudden brightness. Then Bess gasped. The strange sounds were now louder than ever, but there was nobody there! The basement was empty, except for the usual pieces of old furniture and boxes.

"I don't get it," Bess whispered. "There isn't anyone here, so who's making all that noise?"

Nancy didn't answer her right away. Slowly, an idea was taking shape in her mind. After a moment, she whispered back, "I think I know why we can hear the intruders, but we can't see them."

"What are you talking about?" Bess asked in a confused tone.

Nancy pointed at the wall where the sounds were coming from. "I think there's a hidden room behind that wall—one that everybody's forgotten about. Well, almost everybody."

The idea of a secret room made a lot of sense to Nancy. The more she thought about it, the surer she was that this room was where the gold was hidden. That meant that the intruders behind the wall probably weren't Jim and Francesca Rollins after all. Could it be Ethan, Holly, and Kristin who were rummaging through that room?

Nancy listened for a moment. Were those three finding the fortune at this very moment?

The thought worried Nancy. She had to find that secret spot—and she had to find it *now!*

She hurried over to the far side of the basement. A large, old-fashioned cast-iron stove stood in front of the wall. Boxes, books, and other odds and ends were piled on top of the stove. Nancy started pulling objects from the pile and placing them quietly on the concrete floor.

"What are you doing?" asked Bess.

"I think the gold is hidden in a secret room behind this stove," Nancy answered, keeping her voice low.

"What!" exclaimed Bess. "I can't believe it's been there all the time!"

"Help me get this stuff off the stove," Nancy said to her. "We have to get to that room and stop the intruders before they get away with the gold. I just hope we can move the stove away from the wall," she added breathlessly.

The girls worked as quickly as they could. Nancy could almost feel her rivals on the other side of the wall—and the image of them making off with the gold kept flashing through her brain. Ethan, Holly, and Kristin might be in the room stealing Joanna and Josh's inheritance.

Nancy struggled to lift a heavy box, packed to the brim with dishes.

"I just *know* I'm right about the secret hiding place," Nancy whispered. "I searched this basement pretty thoroughly yesterday, but it didn't occur to me that there might be a hidden room behind the wall."

"That makes sense," Bess answered, moving another box. "After all, how could you possibly have known to look behind the stove?"

"Ugh," Nancy groaned, straining to pull a huge, old-fashioned record player off the pile. Then she lost her grip. The record player came tumbling down, just missing Nancy and crashing to the floor.

"Nancy!" said Bess. "Are you okay?"

"I'm fine," Nancy said reassuringly. Then she stood still and listened. The scraping sounds had stopped! Now there was another sound—running footsteps. Whoever had been back there was getting away!

Suddenly Bess and Nancy heard a small, sleepy voice ask, "Bess? Can I have a drink of water?"

The girls turned around to see Josh standing at the top of the stairs. He was rubbing his eyes.

"Josh!" Bess said, hurrying upstairs to the little boy. She knelt down and put her arms around him. "What are you doing out of bed?"

"Noises woke me up," said Josh. He gave a huge yawn. "Can I have a drink of water?" he repeated.

"Of course you can," Bess said soothingly, leading Josh into the kitchen.

Nancy stayed in the basement for a moment, staring at the wall behind the stove. It upset her to think that the searchers might have gotten away with the gold. But their footsteps had been light and quick. If the intruders had been carrying a large amount of gold, they would have moved more slowly. Gold was very heavy. Joanna's fortune was probably still safe—at least for now.

Bess came back downstairs. "I put Josh back

to bed," she told Nancy. "I think those noises frightened him a little."

Nancy nodded. "We'd better put off our search until tomorrow," she said. "Anyway," she added, "I don't think our 'friends' will be back tonight."

"We scared them off, that's for sure," Bess replied, grinning.

Linking their arms together, the girls turned and started up the stairs. When they got to the top, Nancy flicked the light switch, throwing the cellar back into darkness.

When Joanna came home later that evening, Nancy and Bess told her about the secret room. Joanna was excited, but she insisted they wait until tomorrow to search for it.

"The gold has been there all this time," she said to the girls as they were leaving. "One more night won't hurt."

Nancy hoped Joanna was right.

The morning sun streamed into Bess's bedroom. Nancy stretched sleepily and blinked her eyes against the strong light. "Mmm," Bess murmured contentedly from the other bed.

The night before, Nancy had decided to stay at Bess's instead of going back to the Mortmain mansion to pick up her car. Bess had offered to drive Nancy home, but with Nancy's father and Hannah being away, Nancy knew it would be more fun to spend the night at Bess's than to stay alone in an empty house. Besides, Bess's house was closer to the mansion than Nancy's, so staying there had made perfect sense.

Now Nancy knew she had a big job ahead of her. Last night, she'd phoned her other best friend, George Fayne, who had just gotten back from a camping trip with her parents. Nancy had hoped that George would be able to help her and Bess search for the hidden room. George had eagerly agreed to help out. She would be coming over to Bess's that morning.

Nancy leaned back against her pillow and thought about Ethan, Holly, and Kristin. What would their next move be? Would they go back to the hidden room in Joanna's basement? Nancy didn't think they had found the gold in the room, so they probably wouldn't go back there—at least for now. It was more likely they'd try searching other places on their part of the map first.

The jangle of Bess's bedside phone cut into Nancy's thoughts. Bess reached over sleepily and picked it up on the third ring. "Mm— hello?" she said. Bess listened for a moment. "Oh, hi, Hannah," she said finally. "Yes, Nancy's right here." She leaned toward her friend and handed her the phone.

"Hannah?" Nancy said into the phone. "What's up? Did you just get home?"

Hannah's words tumbled over one another,

and she sounded upset. Nancy had a hard time figuring out exactly what she was saying.

"Hannah, calm down," Nancy urged. "Tell me what's happening."

She heard Hannah take a deep breath. "Nancy, there's been another one of those awful robberies," she said. "And this time, they broke into our house!"

8

A Grave Discovery

Nancy knelt down and studied the tire tracks that ran across the Drews' front lawn. She nodded. "It's definitely the Rollinses," she said as she stood up. "Same type of truck—or at least the same type of tires."

"What a couple of creeps," George Fayne said angrily. She and Bess were first cousins, but they were totally different types. George was tall, slim, and athletic, with short brown hair and brown eyes. Unlike her cousin, George wasn't at all nervous around spooky cemeteries or in thieves' hideouts. But despite their differences, the cousins were good friends.

George had shown up at Bess's house soon after Nancy had received Hannah's call about the robbery. Nancy had dressed quickly, and Bess had driven them to the Drews'. On the way to the house, Nancy had filled George in on the two cases.

The police had been to the house earlier. Hannah had given them a full report; then Nancy had told them her theory about the tire tracks. They had written everything down and left. Nancy had double-checked the tire tracks after the police were gone.

The girls went back into Nancy's house, where the thieves had made off with everything of value. They'd stolen the family's computer, stereo system, TV, and VCR. Every piece of Nancy's jewelry was gone—all she had left were the emerald stud earrings she was wearing.

The thieves had really torn the place up. They'd thrown things around, ripped down curtains, and broken two kitchen chairs. Nancy's room had been hit worst of all. It looked as though a tornado had whirled through it.

Sadly Nancy fingered the earrings. They had belonged to her mother. The thieves had also taken the necklace and bracelet that matched the earrings. Unless Nancy could recover the stolen things, those treasured mementos were gone for good.

Nancy shook her head and sighed. "These robbers aren't just greedy. They're vicious."

Bess put her arm around her friend. "It's awful, Nancy."

"What did the police say?" George wanted to know.

"They told me that after the burglary was over, a man called the police to say he'd seen the robbers from the house across the street."

"What!" exclaimed George. "He actually saw them?"

Nancy nodded. "He said he saw a light-colored van drive up to our house. A young man and woman got out and headed around the back of the house. There was enough light from the street lamp for the witness to see that the woman had short brown hair and was wearing a denim jumpsuit. That fits the description of Francesca Rollins. And I saw her wearing a jumpsuit on the news the other night."

"But why didn't the eyewitness call the police right away?" Bess asked.

"He's from out of town," answered Nancy. "He's house-sitting for the couple across the street. He probably just assumed that the man and woman lived in our house."

"That proves the Rollinses pulled off this robbery, too," George said. "The man identified the crooks."

"Right," said Nancy. "The tire tracks point to them, too. Then there's the way the locks were jimmied. The robbers scouted out the house to make sure no one would be home. And the robbery at Bess's house was carried out in exactly the same way."

"But what about the vandalism?" George said. "And the fact that your house is nowhere near the target area?"

Nancy nodded. "Those are two things that make this break-in different," she said thoughtfully. Nancy paused for a moment, then said, "You know, I have a strange feeling that this wasn't just a simple robbery. I think it was also a warning."

Bess and George stared at her in surprise.

"But why are the Rollinses trying to warn you?" Bess asked in a bewildered tone. "They don't know you're on their trail or that we found one of their hiding places."

"I think they *do* know," replied Nancy. "Somehow they must have figured out that I've been tracking them. Maybe they saw us leaving the cabin in the woods. Or maybe they came across the information some other way. Anyway, I'm positive they pulled this break-in to scare me off. Why else would they have put so much work into trashing *my* room in particular? And most of all, what other reason could they have for moving out of their usual area of operations and coming clear across town—unless they wanted to terrify *me?*"

George let out a low whistle. "Nancy, this is getting dangerous!"

"I know," Nancy agreed, "but let's not get too worried about it. The three of us have been

79

in tight spots before. Right now I just want to get this robbery case tied up."

George grinned. "I'm with you, Nancy. Let's go find these creeps and tie *them* up."

Bess nodded. "I've got a few nasty words for whoever messed up your house and mine." She added quickly, "After they're in police custody, that is."

George shot her cousin an amused glance. Then she turned to Nancy. "What's our next move?"

Nancy looked at George, then at Bess. "I know I asked you guys to help me search that hidden room in Joanna's basement today, and we've definitely got to do that soon, or else the other people who are looking for the gold will get there first. But let's put that on hold for now. I think we've got a good chance of finding all Dad's and my stolen stuff, but we have to get a move on."

"Where are we going?" asked Bess.

"We're going back to that shack in the woods—the one where I found your earring. That's the place I want to search this morning. We just might get lucky and catch up with my things there."

"Oh, no," Bess said, groaning. "Not that creepy old cabin again! Nancy, the Rollinses might be there!"

"What about all those nasty things you

wanted to say to them?" George asked her teasingly.

"Don't worry, Bess," said Nancy. "We'll be super-careful."

"Okay, okay," Bess said, sighing. "Let's get it over with."

They made two detours on the way to the woods. One was to the Mortmain mansion to pick up Nancy's car. The other was to Bess's house. They left Bess's car there, and Nancy drove to the dirt road at the edge of the woods.

Nancy stopped her car at the beginning of the road. The three friends got out of the car. "Let's go," said George. "I'm dying to get inside that cabin and see if the Rollinses stashed the stolen goods there." She jogged off toward the shack.

Nancy and Bess hurried after George. Soon they had covered the distance down the road to the cabin.

"Over here," said Nancy. She led her friends to the loose board in the back of the shack. Moments later, they had all slid inside under the loose board. Nancy went to the wall on which the shapeless old tree had been painted. She knelt down and opened the trapdoor.

"Wow," George commented, peering into the room below. "It sure is dark down there."

"Not for long," Nancy told them. She reached into her purse, pulled out her little flashlight, and shone it down into the room. All the beam picked up was the dirt of the earthen floor. The room was totally empty.

"Uh-oh. Looks as though we missed them again," Bess murmured softly.

"Not necessarily," Nancy replied. "We thought the place was empty last time, too. Then I found your earring, half buried in the dirt."

She handed George the flashlight and brushed a lock of hair from her forehead. Then she gently lowered herself into the darkness. Soon she had disappeared through the trapdoor. Her friends squinted, trying to see what Nancy was doing.

"Hand me the light, please," Nancy said. She reached up and felt George place the flashlight in her palm.

Nancy refused to feel disappointed as she shone the light around the empty room. After all, maybe the thieves had left a clue.

Studying the ground carefully, Nancy made her way across the dirt floor. She steadied herself, letting one hand trail against the earthen wall. Her flashlight made a tiny pool of light in the darkness.

"Do you see anything?" George's voice echoed down to her.

"Not yet," Nancy replied. Now she *was* starting to feel a little frustrated. It was just the same damp, empty room as the last time, but minus one gold earring now. The wall felt muddy as her hand moved slowly across its surface.

Then suddenly Nancy felt something harder than packed dirt against her fingers. She pressed her hand against the wall. The surface felt like wood. She aimed the flashlight at the wall and nodded. It *was* wood. And on it was a faded grayish drawing of a lumpy, shapeless tree.

Nancy felt a rush of excitement. The tree upstairs had marked a trapdoor. Could there be another door here? She shone the flashlight around the wooden area, looking for a knothole like the one upstairs. After a moment, she found it. She stuck two fingers into the knothole and pulled hard. A low door in the wall swung outward. Nancy found herself staring into a dark, narrow passageway.

"Bess? George! Come down here," Nancy cried breathlessly. "I've found something incredible!" Instantly, she could hear scrabbling sounds as her friends climbed down into the room.

"You were right. This *is* incredible!" George said as she and Bess stared into the passageway.

The three friends looked at one another. "Why don't we find out where it leads?" suggested George.

"I was hoping you'd say that," Nancy said, grinning.

83

"I was hoping you wouldn't," muttered Bess. "If I die of fright, just send my body back to my folks," she added jokingly, as the three of them started slowly down the dark passageway.

The passageway was so narrow that the girls had to walk in single file. Nancy was in the lead, shining the flashlight on the muddy ground.

"Stick close, you guys," she whispered. "The thieves might be somewhere around here."

"Oh, great," Bess said weakly.

Nothing happened until they had walked for about a quarter of a mile. Then, as the floor of the passageway began to slope upward, the light picked up a white form at the end of the tunnel. As the girls got closer, they could see that it was a door.

Bess shivered slightly. "Why do I get the feeling there's something horrible and creepy on the other side of that door?" she whispered.

The girls crept up to the door. It was solid stone, and it didn't have a knob. Nancy discovered right away that the door was going to be impossible to open. The slab was just too heavy, even with all three of them pushing or pulling at it.

"There's got to be some way to get this thing open," George said.

Nancy nodded in the darkness. "I'm sure we can figure it out. The secret mechanisms to the other hidden doors were all pretty low-tech. So," she reasoned, "this one probably is, too."

"But the knothole trick isn't going to work with stone," Bess pointed out.

"No, but I've done a little reading about hidden rooms. Long ago, when people had them built, they'd fit the doors into the wall so you couldn't see them too easily. You had to know the right spot to push, and the door would shoot open."

"How do we find the right spot?" George wanted to know.

"We'll have to use trial and error," Nancy replied. She slapped one hand lightly against the top of the door. The stone didn't budge. She moved her hand down a bit and pushed again. Still nothing. By the time she'd gotten almost to the bottom of the door, the muscles in her hand were aching. But when she gave one extra-hard shove, a grinding sound filled the air. Instantly the door swung open.

"All *right*, Nancy!" George said, with a big smile.

The girls peered into the large room beyond the door. It was made completely of marble. A heavy marble box, about six feet long, sat in the center. The white marble walls were covered with ornate stone carvings.

"This type of marble . . ." Nancy murmured thoughtfully. "I'm sure I've seen it before."

"But where?" George asked. "A marble room like this is pretty unusual."

Nancy crept curiously into the room for a better look. George and Bess followed close behind.

Suddenly it hit her. The marble was exactly the same type that had been used to build the Mortmain mausoleum, the hundred-year-old tomb in the center of Shady Glen Cemetery. Nancy could feel her heart sinking to her toes. Could this marble room be *inside* the ancient tomb?

She glanced down at the white stone box. It had to be a coffin! Images of skeletons and ghosts fluttered through her mind. "Guys, I hate to tell you this," she said to her friends, "but we're in a tomb!"

"What!" exclaimed Bess. She turned and started for the door. As she did, a grinding sound ripped through the room. The heavy stone door slammed shut and a hundred years' worth of dust puffed across the floor. Their only escape route from the tomb was sealed off.

"Hey!" Nancy shouted.

She dashed to the stone slab and pounded on it. Then she began the same insistent pressing that had opened the door on the tunnel side.

But after a lot of hard work, the three friends were just as stuck as they'd been before. The door wouldn't budge. There was no way out.

They were trapped in the tomb!

9

Kristin Confesses—Almost

"Now what do we do?" asked George. "No one will ever think of looking for us here."

Bess glanced at the ghostly white stone coffin and shuddered. "I want to get out of here," she said shakily.

Nancy put her arm around Bess's shoulder. "Take it easy, Bess," she said gently. "We'll get out. But it may take a little time."

Nancy looked at George. Even she was frightened, Nancy could tell. Nancy had to admit that she was a little scared, too. Being shut up in here was like being buried alive. Nancy didn't want to think about what would happen if they couldn't find a way out.

Nancy took a few deep, calming breaths. "Okay, guys," she said. "Let's not panic. There has to be another way out of here."

87

She let her gaze wander around the mausoleum. In the dim light, the carvings in the marble seemed to be grinning evilly at her. On one wall, a dragon crouched as if ready to spring. A strange stone bird stared rudely from another wall.

"We're stuck!" Bess said frantically. "We'll never get that door open, and there isn't so much as a chink in the rest of the wall!"

Nancy felt a sudden rush of fear. She wished Bess would calm down. If she didn't, soon they'd *all* start to get panicky, and that wouldn't help them get out of there.

"The walls aren't the only place to look for a way out," Nancy told Bess quietly. Her gaze wandered to the ceiling. A large death's-head, made out of bits of colored glass, grinned at her from above. Nancy stared hard at it. Then, slowly, a smile slid across her face. "I think I just found our escape hatch," she said.

George and Bess looked up at the skull on the ceiling. "A stained-glass skylight!" George said excitedly.

"Right!" Nancy replied, nodding.

"Thank goodness," Bess said with a sigh. "I don't think I can stand to be trapped in here another minute."

The glass was dirty and caked with grime, shutting out most of the bright summer sunlight. Nancy peered at the latch at the bottom of the window. "Luckily, that lock looks pretty

rusty, so it should be easy to break," she told
Bess and George. She took her flashlight out of
her pocket. She could bang the lock open with
that.

"How do we get up there?" Bess wanted to
know.

Nancy pointed to the coffin, which was directly beneath the window.

Bess gulped. "Do we have to?"

"Don't think about what's inside the coffin,"
suggested George. "Just think about all that
great fresh air and sunshine waiting for you
outside!"

"I'll go first," Nancy said. She climbed on
top of the coffin and stood up.

"Perfect!" she said. She was right under the
lock.

As Nancy gave the window a little shake, she
realized she wasn't going to need her flashlight
after all. The window wasn't locked, just
latched shut. It opened easily.

"Great!" said Bess. "Now you won't have to
break the lock."

Nancy nodded slowly. "Yes, but the fact that
this window is open means that someone could
have been here besides us."

"The thieves, probably," suggested George.

"Well, let's not worry about that right now—
at least not until we get out of here," Bess
urged.

Nancy hoisted herself through the open window. With a thankful sigh, she emerged into the daylight. A moment later, Bess's relieved face appeared, and then George climbed out.

"Come on!" Nancy exclaimed, surveying the cemetery from the top of the mausoleum. "It feels great to be out of there!" She inched her way across the roof, then jumped to the ground. Knowing her friends wouldn't be far behind her, she began to run down the hill toward the cemetery exit. The sun on her skin and the breeze through her hair felt great.

Suddenly she stopped short. Up ahead, through the exit, she could see three people getting out of a light blue van. It was Holly Harris, Ethan Davidson, and Kristin! The three teenagers didn't look pleased as they walked toward Nancy. In fact, they looked really angry. Nancy groaned inwardly. Obviously she was in for more trouble with these three.

"You don't listen, do you?" Ethan said as he approached her.

"You just can't take a hint," Kristin added, but Nancy could hear uncertainty in her voice.

"We know you were at the Mortmain mansion yesterday," Holly said. "Snooping around."

Now Nancy had had enough of these three. A wave of anger swept over her as she thought about how they'd planned to jump her when she got to her car. They were nothing but *bullies*.

Nancy glared at each of them in turn. "Yes, I was at the Mortmain mansion yesterday. And I heard every word you said about me staying out of your business—permanently!"

"I meant it," Ethan said menacingly. He raised his hand and balled it into a fist.

"N-no, Ethan, don't!" Kristin said suddenly. "Please don't."

"Shut up, Kristin!" snapped Holly.

Then Nancy spotted Bess and George. They were standing behind Ethan, several feet away.

"You can try to punch me out," Nancy said coldly to Ethan, "but there are two witnesses standing behind you who will see you do it. They'll go to the police, and that will be the end of your 'business'—permanently."

Ethan turned and saw Bess and George. Slowly he dropped his arm to his side.

"Listen, Drew," Ethan said, still trying to sound tough but not doing a very convincing job of it. "We're not going to waste our energy warning you again. Stay out of our way. Or next time it won't be only a warning." With that, he whirled around and strode down the hill, his friends following behind.

George let out a hoot of laughter as she watched them go. "Way to go, Nancy. It's so easy to scare away bullies."

Nancy was still angry. "Yes, they are bullies," she agreed. "They're also selfish, mean, and greedy."

"Well, you've got a couple of friends who definitely aren't going to let Ethan and his crowd bother you," George said, smiling.

"You know, Nancy," Bess said suddenly, "I've been wondering how those three got hold of the other part of the treasure map."

Nancy shook her head. "I don't know. In fact, I don't even have proof that they *do* have it. But we have to assume they do. Otherwise, what could have led them to the Mortmain mansion and the cemetery?"

"Maybe it's time to *get* proof," Bess suggested.

"You're right," Nancy agreed. "We need to find a connection between Ethan, Holly, Kristin, and the wardrobe Joanna sold to the antiques dealer. If we go back to the Curious Cat and talk to Catherine Hansen again, we just might be able to do that."

Nancy turned to Bess and George and gave each of them a big hug.

"Thanks for sticking with me, you guys. Anyway, even though we got locked in the mausoleum, and in spite of the run-in with Ethan and the others, I think we did some really good detecting on the robbery case today."

"What did we learn?" George asked curiously.

"Well," Nancy began, "it's pretty clear now that the Rollinses are avoiding the police by stashing stolen goods in the shack in the woods and in the mausoleum, then removing them when the coast is clear. No one's been able to track them down—yet. But this new information just might help us do it."

"What about the missing gold?" Bess asked.

Nancy sighed. "I'm positive that Ethan, Holly, and Kristin are involved, but I'm not sure how to prove it yet."

The lack of proof was really nagging at Nancy. She definitely needed some evidence before she could confront those three, but she had no clear idea of how to get it.

For the second time in three days, Nancy made her way through the maze of antiques and over to the cash register where Catherine Hansen was standing. It was the middle of the afternoon. Since George was scheduled for lifeguard duty at the pool and Bess was taking Josh to the dentist so that Joanna could get some studying done, Nancy was investigating this lead on her own.

The antiques dealer looked up and smiled. "Oh, hello," she said cheerfully. "Have you decided to buy that beautiful wardrobe after all?"

Nancy shook her head. "I've come about the wardrobe—but not because I want to buy it."

A puzzled expression crossed the antiques dealer's face, but it was instantly replaced by a smile. "Well, I'll be happy to help you with anything I can."

Suddenly a girl's voice from outside cut through the still afternoon. "Mom?" the girl said. "Can I use the car for a few hours?"

There was nothing unusual about the words, but Nancy's heart skipped a beat. She'd heard that voice before, the last time she was here and yesterday in the Mortmain mansion—and today in the cemetery. Kristin's words from earlier in the afternoon echoed through her head: "You just can't take a hint."

So that was it! She'd found the link between the threatening trio and the missing part of the treasure map. Kristin must have searched through Joanna's wardrobe as soon as it had come into the shop—before her mother had had a chance to check it out. She must have found the map part then and shown it to Ethan and Holly. Nancy also figured that Kristin was probably the one who had written that warning note and put it on the windshield of Nancy's car. It had been Kristin, not her mother, who had seen Nancy looking through the wardrobe and gotten nervous. She'd gotten Nancy's name from the guest book, then written the note, hoping it would scare Nancy off the case.

"Mom?" Kristin's voice repeated.

Mrs. Hansen shook her head wearily. "My daughter just won't remember not to shout from the house, no matter how many times I tell her." She sighed. "I'd better talk to her before the whole neighborhood complains." She slipped from behind the counter.

"Uh, can I ask you something first?" Nancy said.

The antiques dealer turned back. "Sure."

Nancy pressed her lips together. "Does your daughter ever help you with your antiques business?" she asked.

Mrs. Hansen nodded. "You bet. I taught her everything I know, and now I think she's got a better nose for antiques than I have," she added proudly. "Actually, she's the one who worked on that wardrobe."

"Mom!" Kristin demanded a third time.

"I'll be back in a moment," Mrs. Hansen told Nancy apologetically. "Have a look around," she said before she hurried outside.

Nancy leaned against the counter and thought about the information she'd just learned. What should she do now? Confront Kristin? Or would it be better not to get into another potentially explosive situation?

Nancy heard someone enter the antiques store behind her. She turned around. Kristin's angry face stared at her from the doorway. She was wearing a black leather jacket, even though it was a hot summer day. It was pretty difficult to believe that this tough-acting teen would spend hours working on antiques with her mother.

"What are you doing here?" Kristin demanded. She was trying to sound hard, but her voice was trembling slightly.

Suddenly Nancy realized something—Kristin was terrified of her! "Kristin, I know about the map," Nancy said evenly. "The tunnel, the mausoleum, the warning note—everything."

Kristin shrank back as if Nancy had slapped her. "They—they made me do it," she gasped. "I didn't want to be in on it at all. But they said they'd tell my mother about the time I got caught shoplifting if I didn't go along with them. I—I didn't want my mother to know about the shoplifting."

Nancy remembered how Kristin had acted in the cemetery when Ethan was about to start throwing punches, but she'd never expected the girl to break down like this. All of a sudden, there was no sign of any toughness. Kristin was just a frightened kid.

Something about all this didn't make sense. Kristin was confessing as if she'd committed a crime, but there was nothing illegal about searching for gold. If they found it, the worst that would happen to them was that they'd have to return it to its rightful owner. Was Kristin worried about the threats the three of them had made against Nancy?

"Why don't you tell me what's bothering you," Nancy said quietly.

Kristin's face seemed to quiver, and for a moment, Nancy thought she was going to burst into tears. All at once, though, her expression changed from fear to anger. She glared at Nancy.

"Everyone thinks you're so honest!" Kristin spat out. "But I know the truth. You're just as greedy as Ethan and Holly!"

Nancy stared at Kristin in disbelief.

"If you were really all that trustworthy," Kristin continued in a shrill voice, "you would have gone to the police already. But you haven't. My guess is, you want in on the deal. Right?"

Nancy shook her head slowly. The other girl's words just didn't make any sense. "Kristin, I don't know what you're talking about."

Kristin continued to glare at Nancy. "Don't play innocent with me," she muttered, but Nancy could see the girl's eyes fill with tears.

"I'm not playing—" Nancy began.

Kristin cut her off. "If money will keep you quiet, you've got it," she whispered tearfully. "I'm willing to do anything to cover this up. Anything!"

10

A Startling Revelation

Nancy stared into Kristin's frightened eyes. She couldn't believe what she had just heard. And yet it was true. Kristin was trying to bribe her! The idea was so ridiculous that Nancy almost laughed.

The strangest thing of all was that Nancy had absolutely no idea *what* Kristin was trying to keep her from revealing. Were Kristin and the others involved in more than just a treasure hunt? Somehow Nancy had to get Kristin to tell her why she was so worried and desperate. She had to win Kristin's trust.

"Kristin," Nancy said quietly, "why don't we sit down and talk about this?"

A satisfied look appeared in Kristin's eyes. "Then I was right! You *do* want money," she said triumphantly.

Nancy shook her head. "No, that's not it. But

I'd hate to see you get into trouble just because Ethan and Holly blackmailed you into doing all this." Kristin narrowed her eyes. "I promise I won't reveal anything you tell me—unless it's absolutely necessary."

As soon as the words were out of her mouth, Nancy realized she'd made a mistake.

"I knew it!" Kristin burst out. "You're looking for more information, something you can blab to the cops." She scowled at Nancy. "Holly's right. You're just a teacher's pet who's gotten too nosy for her own good!" With that, Kristin turned abruptly and stormed out of the store.

"Kristin!" Nancy called after her. But it was no use. She'd blown her chance. With a sigh, Nancy made her way through the maze of antiques and out of the shop. She headed across the lawn to her car.

Nancy got into her car feeling annoyed with herself for having missed an opportunity to get more information from Kristin. What she needed right now was a friend to talk to about the case. If she hurried over to Joanna's, maybe she could catch Bess before her friend took Josh to the dentist.

Nancy also wanted to look for the hidden room in Joanna's basement. The events of the day seemed to have put the search for the gold into the background. When Nancy pulled into the Williamses' driveway, she saw Bess and

Josh coming down the porch steps. Bess was holding Josh's hand, and he was smiling up at her. When Bess saw Nancy, she hurried Josh down the steps.

"Nancy! What are you doing here?" she said.

Nancy got out of the car and slammed the door behind her. "I need to talk about the gold investigation," she explained. "I thought maybe you could help me figure a few things out."

Bess let out a laugh. "*Me?* I'm hardly your best bet as a detective. But sure, if you think talking will help, go ahead. Josh and I were planning to go to the playground before his dentist appointment, but I don't think Josh will mind staying here instead." She smiled at Josh. "Why don't you ride your bike in front of the house for a little while before we go to the dentist?"

"Okay," said Josh. Bess let go of his hand and he ran off.

Nancy and Bess walked to the front porch and settled on the top step. For a moment, they watched Josh as he headed down the walk on his bike.

"He's a nice little boy," Nancy commented.

Bess nodded. "He's my favorite kid to babysit for," she said. "Even if he did make me read him all his Roboman comic books today!" she added with a smile.

"So what's the matter?" Bess wanted to know. "You look almost as upset as you did when you found out the Rollinses had broken into your house."

Nancy sighed. "Actually, it's the other case—Joanna's lost gold—that's bothering me right now." Quickly she filled her friend in on her most recent conversation with Kristin Hansen.

"That's pretty weird," Bess commented after Nancy finished.

"Yeah. It's left me with a lot to think about," Nancy agreed. "For one thing, I know for sure now that Kristin and the others really do have the other part of the map, because when I mentioned it, Kristin didn't even seem surprised. In fact, she acted as though it was completely natural for me to know about it."

Bess's eyes wandered from Josh to Nancy. "So they really are on the trail of Joanna's gold."

"Right. And since our part of the map doesn't show the spot where the gold is actually hidden, I just have to assume that the hiding place is marked on Kristin's half of the map."

"Uh-oh. Now I see why you're so upset," Bess murmured. "If Kristin, Holly, and Ethan learned where the gold was hidden, they've probably found it already."

Nancy shook her head in frustration. "But if Ethan and his crowd have found the gold already, why are they still hanging around the Mortmain house and the cemetery? And anoth-

101

er thing—how did they realize the Mortmain mansion figured in the hunt at all? That was marked on *our* half of the map!"

"Then they probably haven't found the gold after all!" Bess said excitedly.

"Not yet, anyway," Nancy said. "But I'm sure they're still looking. I don't know how close they are to figuring out where it is, but there's one thing I *do* know: I'm going to find it first." She stood up quickly.

"Where are you going?" asked Bess, looking up at her curiously.

"That secret room in Joanna's basement," Nancy decided. "Remember, we haven't searched that room yet."

"Think you can handle it yourself?" Bess asked, looking at her watch. "I've got to get Josh to the dentist." She glanced at the little boy. He had stopped riding his bike. Now he was in the front yard, kicking around a soccer ball.

"No problem," Nancy said. "Maybe Joanna can take a break from her studying to help."

"Hey, Josh, let's go," Bess called to the five-year-old. "We can stop at the playground on our way back from the dentist. Okay?"

"Yay!" Josh shouted, running to Bess. The two of them waved to Nancy as they hurried out the front gate.

Nancy turned to the door and let the rooster door knocker fall. A moment later, she heard footsteps in the house. Then the door opened, and Joanna appeared. "Nancy! Come in!" she said warmly, opening the door wide. "I was just about to take a study break."

Nancy smiled at her and said, "Do you have time right now to look for the secret room in your basement?"

"Are you kidding?" said Joanna. "Of course I have time! Do you think that's where the gold is hidden?" she asked.

"It's a good possibility," Nancy replied cautiously.

"Well, what are we waiting for?" Joanna said with a grin. "Let's go check it out!"

Nancy and Joanna made their way down the cellar stairs. When they reached the bottom steps, Joanna gave Nancy's arm a squeeze. "After wondering and guessing all this time," she whispered, "we'll finally find out if Laura Atwood's legacy is for real!"

Nancy smiled. "Come on. We've got work to do." She stepped over to the stove that stood against the wall. Joanna followed her.

"You think the hidden room is behind the stove?" Joanna asked.

Nancy nodded. "That's where Bess and I heard the sounds coming from last night." She gripped the back of the cast-iron stove. Joanna grabbed the front corner. The two of them tugged and pushed, but the stove wouldn't budge.

"We're not giving up," Joanna said between her teeth. "Push harder, Nancy."

They tugged and pushed as hard as they could. Finally the stove began to move away from the wall. With a little more effort, Joanna and Nancy managed to move the stove far enough away so that there was a good-size gap between the stove and the wall.

Nancy looked at the wall and blinked in amazement. In front of her was a faded drawing of a lumpy, shapeless tree.

Nancy couldn't take her eyes off the drawing. It was the same tree she'd seen on the wall of the cabin in the woods and in the room below. That meant that the two places were connected—the cabin she'd traced to the robbery case and the secret room in Joanna's basement.

Kneeling, Nancy ran her hand along the cement wall. She felt a crack, and then her fingers traced the outline of a door. A tremendous shove in the right spot should send the whole thing flying open—like the door in the mausoleum. Nancy took a deep breath and threw her weight against the wall. A whole section of it slid back, and she found herself staring into a long dirt passageway just like the one that led from the cabin into the Mortmain mausoleum.

"You did it, Nancy!" exclaimed Joanna. "The gold's got to be back there!" She turned and headed for the stairs. "I'll go get a flash-light," she said excitedly.

Nancy didn't feel as excited as Joanna did. The pieces began to fall into place. All this time she'd been missing the most obvious fact. Her two summer mysteries were really one and the same case.

Nancy remembered that the tree drawing in the cabin was bright red. It looked and felt as though it had been painted fairly recently. The other drawings were a faded grayish color.

Nancy nodded grimly. She was sure now that the Rollinses weren't responsible for the recent string of robberies. All this time, the police—and Nancy herself—had been blaming two innocent people!

Nancy also remembered the robbery at her own house and the way her room had been vandalized. Suddenly she knew who the real thieves were: Ethan Davidson, Holly Harris, and Kristin Hansen. They were out-and-out criminals who'd broken into a dozen homes in less than three weeks!

They'd probably never known about the gold. They'd simply used their part of the map to locate hiding places and secret passageways. The tree in the cabin had been drawn by the thieves to mark the trapdoor. They'd probably marked other hiding places and used those spots to stash the loot they'd stolen. It was a smart plan, guaranteed to fool the police.

So that's why Kristin had acted so frightened. She hadn't been worried about the gold. She thought Nancy knew that she and the others were the thieves.

Then all those warnings weren't just empty threats of a few bullies. Ethan and his gang were playing for keeps. They're out for blood, Nancy realized. *And I'm the target!*

11

Nancy Sets a Trap

Nancy couldn't let herself worry about the danger she might be in. Somehow she had to get proof that Ethan, Holly, and Kristin were the thieves. To do that, she'd have to catch them red-handed in the act of breaking into a house or with the stolen loot.

Nancy fingered one of her emerald earrings thoughtfully. She'd have to set them up. And she'd need to make sure the police were there to see the whole thing happen. That shouldn't be too hard to do. In fact, she had a few ideas already.

Just then, Joanna came back into the basement.

"Well, are you ready to find that gold?" she asked, holding up a large flashlight.

"Look, Joanna," Nancy said, turning to the

other woman, "I know you want to search this passageway. So do I. But I just figured out a way to catch those robbers, and I need your help. I'm going to try to set up a police sting operation."

Joanna smiled at her. "The gold can wait. I'd love to help catch the creeps who robbed you and Bess."

"Great! I'm going to make a few phone calls. All you have to do is take Josh and stay away from home tomorrow night—go someplace safe and out of the way."

"You mean, I won't get to see any of the action?" Joanna said jokingly.

"Don't worry. You will when I find that gold for you!" Nancy turned, then dashed up the stairs, taking them two at a time.

Hurrying into the living room, she picked up the phone and quickly hit the numbers for the police station. The front desk operator answered.

"This is Nancy Drew. I need to speak to Chief McGinnis, please."

"Hello, Ms. Drew," the operator replied. "No problem. I'll put you through to the chief immediately."

A moment later, the chief's rough voice greeted Nancy. "Hey there, private eye. Got any interesting leads for me?"

Nancy smiled into the mouthpiece. "You bet! Want to catch those robbers?"

Nancy could hear the chief laughing on the other end of the line. "Are you kidding?" he said. "Of course I want to catch the Rollinses. This case has been driving us crazy!"

Nancy thought for a moment. Should she tell Chief McGinnis that the Rollinses weren't responsible for the robberies? If she did, he might not believe her. Much as the police chief liked and respected Nancy, she knew he still thought of her as an amateur. It was possible he wouldn't send out any officers to help her if she told him her real theory.

Nancy made a quick decision. She wouldn't tell the chief now. He'd find out who the real thieves were soon enough.

"Okay, here's my plan," she said into the phone. "Tomorrow night we'll need a couple of officers outside a cabin in the woods I know about. I found one of Bess Marvin's stolen earrings there. A few more officers should be stationed at the Mortmain mausoleum in the old cemetery," she continued. "The thieves will stash their loot in one of those places."

"And how do you know there'll be a robbery tomorrow night?" the chief asked.

Nancy smiled to herself. "Don't worry about that. I'll take care of everything."

"Hmph," the chief said gruffly. "And I suppose you intend to be at one of those places, too?"

Before Nancy could reply, the chief said,

109

"It's too dangerous, Nancy. Those people aren't going to go back to jail quietly."

Nancy rolled her eyes. She had expected him to warn her off. "You're going to need me on the scene," she said. "Tell me, how many officers can you spare?"

The phone was silent for a moment as Chief McGinnis did a quick calculation of the available officers. "Three," he said finally.

"We're going to need two people at each spot. With your three officers, I'd be the perfect fourth." Nancy took a deep breath. "Come on, Chief. You know I can handle myself." There was a pause. Nancy heard the chief give a huge sigh.

"Okay, Nancy, you're in," he told her. "You'd probably show up at the stakeout anyway, even if I told you not to. But I want you to know the exact arrangements when it's all set up."

"Great, Chief McGinnis, and thanks a lot!"

Nancy hung up and a huge smile spread over her face. It was going to work. Now all she had to do was arrange a robbery.

Nancy picked up the phone again and punched out a second number. The phone rang three times before a girl's voice answered.

"Hi, Kristin, this is Nancy Drew."

"Why are you calling?" Kristin replied nervously.

"I just wanted to tell you that I'll take your offer," Nancy told her crisply.

"My offer?" Kristin repeated. "You mean the one about giving you money to keep quiet?"

"That's it," Nancy replied. She hoped that she sounded convincing. "Only it's not money I want. I'm looking for jewelry. Good-quality stuff. And I happen to know someone who has the most incredible emerald earrings. I saw them last time I was baby-sitting for her."

"I knew it," Kristin said scornfully. "You're just as crooked as we are. That goody-goody private-eye act is just a pose."

"Look, Kristin," Nancy said coldly. "Just make sure I get those emeralds."

Kristin paused. Then she said, "Don't worry, you will." Nancy quickly gave Kristin Joanna's name and address and told her where to find the earrings. Then she hung up.

She smiled, took off her emerald earrings, and planted them in Joanna's jewelry box. Everything was set up for the next night. It couldn't fail.

The next evening, Nancy was huddled under the overhang of the mausoleum roof with Officer Marquez of the River Heights police force. Rain was pouring down steadily. Nancy and the officer were sitting on the narrow entrance space, trying their best to keep dry.

"Just our luck," Nancy said. "Beautiful weather for almost a week straight. Then we get this awful storm on the one night we've got to sit outside for a stakeout."

Nancy and the tall, dark-haired police officer sat silently for a moment. The only sounds they could hear were the pounding of the rain against the mausoleum roof and an occasional crash of distant thunder. Every once in a while, streaks of lightning lit up the sky.

Nancy was miserable. Her jeans were soaked and her nylon rain jacket was damp and sticking to her skin.

"You think those crooks will show?" Marquez asked, breaking the silence. He gathered his police-issue rain poncho more tightly around him. "It's almost eleven. Maybe they decided not to go for the bait."

Nancy wiped off a stream of water that was slowly making its way down the back of her neck. "I'd hate to think of us waiting here half the night for nothing. Let's give them another half-hour, okay?"

"Okay," the officer agreed, but Nancy had the feeling he would have been all too happy to leave the soggy cemetery for someplace warm and dry.

Nancy and Officer Marquez sat and waited.

Somewhere nearby a bird screeched. Thunder rumbled in the distance.

Then Nancy heard it. It was coming from farther down the cemetery hill—a girl's strangled scream. "Help!" The cry pierced through the sound of the rain. "Help!"

12

Buried Alive!

Officer Marquez was on his feet instantly. "Where'd those screams come from?" he muttered, scanning the cemetery from left to right.

"Help!" The cry was louder this time.

Marquez turned to Nancy. "You stay here," he said to her. "I'm going to check this out." Then he raced down the rain-soaked hill.

Nancy jumped up, too, watching Officer Marquez run. She had to stifle the urge to rush after him. But he was right, she did have to stay here. What if Kristin, Holly, and Ethan showed up right at this moment? It was important to have a witness waiting here when they did.

Nancy looked up at the sky. Wouldn't it ever stop raining? The pounding of the raindrops was getting on her nerves.

Five minutes passed, then ten. The cries for

114

help had stopped, but Officer Marquez still wasn't back. Maybe the screams had led him out of the cemetery. Nancy sighed. If Ethan and the others did show up, she hoped the officer would be there to catch them. The whole point of the operation was to have a police witness.

All of a sudden, Nancy felt a hand cover her mouth roughly. Then an arm wrapped itself around her throat in a stranglehold. Two more hands pinned her arms behind her. By twisting her hands sharply, Nancy managed to free them from her captor's grasp. She reached up and tore the hand away from her mouth.

"Marquez! Help!" she shouted. She struggled to get out of the stranglehold, but it was no use. The person was gripping her too tightly.

"He's gone," a familiar voice whispered in her ear. It was Ethan Davidson. He laughed softly. "I don't think you'll be seeing him again."

Nancy felt her arms being pinned behind her back again. "Kristin's leading that cop on a wild-goose chase that'll take hours to finish," she heard Holly Harris say.

"Scream all you want to," said Ethan. "No one will hear you." He motioned to Holly. "Tie her wrists," he ordered. "And make sure the knot is really tight."

Quickly Holly did as she was told. "You

didn't really think we'd fall into your little trap, did you?" Holly said as she worked. "Face it, we're just too smart for you!"

When Holly had finished, Nancy wriggled her hands to see if she could loosen the rope that was binding her wrists, but Holly had tied the knot too expertly. There was no way Nancy would be able to get free.

Ethan had removed his arm from Nancy's throat. Nancy got ready to throw her weight against Holly. If she could do it in a swift, sudden movement, she'd catch Holly off guard. With Holly on the ground and Ethan momentarily startled, she might be able to run away.

As if Ethan had read her thoughts, he said, "Don't try anything funny, Ms. Detective. I'm watching you very carefully." He held up something in front of Nancy's face. With a sinking feeling, Nancy saw that it was a knife. "Okay," Ethan said menacingly. "Let's go."

Go where? Nancy wondered. To some spot in the woods? She was sure they wouldn't take her to the cabin. If they knew about the police setup, then they probably knew that officers were staking out the cabin.

Somehow Nancy had to stall them until Officer Marquez got back. Even though Holly seemed sure he'd be gone for a long time, Nancy didn't think he'd continue to chase Kristin much longer. His real job was back here, and he knew it.

"You know, that *was* pretty smart of you to figure out this trap," Nancy said, trying to keep her voice calm and pleasant. "How did you do it?"

Ethan smiled. "It was easy," he said with a smirk. "After Kristin called and told us you wanted to cut yourself in on a robbery, Holly remembered those emerald earrings you always wear. Then we just put two and two together and decided you were planning to set us up."

"Wow," Nancy replied, looking at Ethan and Holly admiringly. "You two really outsmarted me." She glanced toward the hill. Where was Officer Marquez? He should have been back by now.

Holly was watching her closely. "This little creep is trying to stall us until that cop gets here," she said to Ethan.

"Don't worry," Ethan said reassuringly. "I gave Kristin instructions on how to keep him chasing her. If she just follows directions, we'll be fine. He'll be tracing her cries for help all over the neighborhood. He'll never get back—at least, not in time to save our friend here." He laughed nastily.

"What are you going to do with her?" Holly asked.

"Just put her out of the way for a while—*way* out of the way."

Nancy felt a shiver go up her spine.

What horrible fate was Ethan planning for her?

"And after she's taken care of, we can afford to stop working for a while. Maybe take a little vacation out of town. The police won't be able to prove we're the thieves. And no one's going to connect us with a missing person."

"What about Kristin?" Holly wanted to know. "Can we trust her to keep her mouth shut?"

Nancy was beginning to see that Holly didn't have as much trouble with the idea of dumping her as she did with the possibility that they might not get away with their whole operation.

Ethan frowned. "Kristin will keep quiet—if she knows what's good for her." He scowled at Nancy. "We've wasted enough time standing here talking. Let's go." He grabbed Nancy's arm and held it in an ironlike grip.

"Okay, get onto that mausoleum roof," Ethan ordered.

Nancy hesitated for a moment, desperately trying to think of a way to escape.

Ethan pushed her forward. "Get going!" he snapped. "I'm going to untie your hands now, but don't bother trying to get away. Holly and I will be sticking real close to you."

After Nancy's hands were freed, the three of them hoisted themselves up to the top of the tomb. Ethan clicked open the stained-glass skylight and motioned for Holly to jump in. Then he pushed Nancy inside.

This is it, Nancy thought. For one tiny instant, she was going to be more than an arm's length away from Ethan. If she timed it just right, she might be able to gain control of the situation.

Nancy stared down into the tomb. It was dark inside, but she could just make out Holly's shape next to the coffin. Aiming her body, she leapt into the black, empty space.

Holly groaned as Nancy's weight came crashing against her. "Ethan!" Holly screamed.

As Nancy struggled with Holly in the dim light, she heard Ethan jump down from the roof. She spun around to face him, but she'd been too slow. He grabbed her arms and flashed the knife in front of her face.

"Don't try anything like that again!" he said furiously. By then Holly had lit a lantern and the whole tomb was bathed in a flickering, ghostly light. Suddenly Nancy saw that the stone cover of the coffin was open. They couldn't really mean to put her in there!

Ethan watched Nancy stare in horror at the open coffin. "No one's ever been buried here. We found that out when we looked inside after our first robbery. The coffin made a great storage place for the loot we stole. And now it's going to be your new home!"

119

For the first time, Holly appeared uncertain. "Look, Ethan, are you sure this is a good idea? I mean, isn't there another way we could get her not to talk? We could pay her off, or—"

"Shut up!" Ethan interrupted angrily. "This is the only way to be absolutely *sure* she won't talk."

"Okay, but I still don't like it," Holly muttered.

Meanwhile, Nancy was trying to stay calm enough to figure out a way to escape from this horrible situation. After all, she'd been in tough spots before.

Ethan gave her a rough shove. "All right, get in that coffin!" he said harshly.

Nancy bit her lip thoughtfully. If she didn't do what Ethan said, he might finish her off right here. But if she got into the coffin, there was a chance she could escape later, after Ethan and Holly had left the mausoleum.

Nancy forced herself to step to the coffin. Then, very slowly, she got inside and lay down.

Looking up, she could see Ethan grinning at her cruelly. Holly stood beside him looking much more uncertain than her accomplice. Together, they began inching the lid closed, slowly shutting out the light.

Then the top fell with a thud, and Nancy was left in total darkness.

13

The Gold Is Found!

Nancy lay in the darkness. It was so quiet she could hear her heart pounding inside her chest.

She waited until she was sure Holly and Ethan had left the mausoleum. Then she reached up and pushed against the coffin's lid, straining with all her strength. It didn't budge. She pushed harder, this time with her legs as well as her arms. Nothing.

Nancy knew she was in a bad position to move that lid. Because she was lying down, she had no leverage. If she'd had a little more leg room, she could have knelt inside the coffin. Then she would have been able to use all the strength of her back, as well as her arms, to push away the coffin's top. But there wasn't space to move around.

Nancy continued to push up at the lid. After

121

about half an hour, she lay back, exhausted. But she couldn't give up! She *had* to get out of there. She'd just give herself a little rest, then try pushing again—harder.

Nancy concentrated, trying to relax her tired muscles. She lay completely still and breathed very lightly. She had to avoid using up the small amount of oxygen inside the tomb.

As Nancy rested, some questions formed in her mind. Why did the Mortmains build a huge, elaborate mausoleum and then not bury anybody in the coffin? And why include two escape tunnels, one to Joanna's house and one to the cabin in the woods? The whole setup was very strange.

But, Nancy reasoned, if this coffin was never meant for burial, it clearly had been built for some other purpose. Maybe as a hiding place. What could the Mortmains have wanted to hide in here?

But if it was true that the Mortmains had intended to use the coffin as a hiding place, there just might be a hidden entrance to it, one like the huge stone door in the room outside.

Nancy ran her hand down one side of the coffin. Carefully, she pressed along the length of stone exactly as she had when she'd found the other secret doors. But this time, there was no trigger mechanism to be found. Both sides of the coffin were completely solid. So were the walls at Nancy's feet and head.

Nancy refused to give up. Maybe, just maybe, she hadn't looked in the right spot for that secret panel. Inching herself over onto her stomach, Nancy began to press along the bottom of the coffin.

Then it happened. Without warning, the floor gave way and Nancy fell downward! "Ouch!" Nancy cried as her shin hit something hard hidden beneath the false bottom of the coffin.

Okay, Nancy thought. Now all I've got to do is find the crawl space that leads out of here. She tried to feel along the walls of the hidden space she'd discovered, but something kept getting in her way. It felt like a box. And there was no opening! None. Feeling just a little frantic, Nancy ran her hand along each wall a second time, but she still couldn't find an opening in one of the walls. She was just as stuck as she'd been before she discovered the false bottom.

Nancy looked up into the coffin. When she was lying inside it, she hadn't been able to budge the lid. But now there was space to kneel inside the coffin. The new position gave her much more leverage. This time she might be able to push the lid off.

Nancy knelt and pressed her hands against the coffin's lid. "One, two, three, *heave*," she counted out loud as she began to push. The lid made a grinding sound as it scraped against the top of the coffin. "Keep it up," Nancy urged herself. "If you keep up the pressure, it *has* to move."

After one extra push, the lid gave a little leap. It landed with a crash against the coffin again—but a piece of stone had been chipped off, leaving a crack. Nancy slid her fingers into the crack, then used all her strength to shove the top off the coffin. The mausoleum echoed with the deafening sound of the lid as it crashed to the floor. She was out!

Nancy stood up and stretched. The lantern Holly had left behind cast a ghostly glow around the tomb, but Nancy didn't pay attention to the spooky shadows made by the lantern's flickering light. She was too happy to be out of her prison. Now all she had to do was to climb out the skylight and she'd be completely free!

But there was one thing she wanted to check out before she left—that box in the false bottom of the coffin. What was in it? Had Ethan and his gang left some of their stolen loot behind? Or had the box been there for much longer? Was *it* the thing this whole mausoleum had been built to protect?

Nancy went over to the lantern and picked it up. Then she climbed back into the coffin and stepped into the hidden space. She put the lantern down next to the box. The box was made of wood and it had no lock. She bent down and lifted the lid off. The box was lined with velvet. And on the velvet was a jumble of metal trinkets and coins. In the light of the lantern, the objects shone with a golden glow. Nancy pulled one large piece—a necklace—out of the pile.

Suddenly she realized what she was holding. It was no ordinary necklace. It was made out of solid gold, as were the other things in the box. The valuable items in this box were worth a fortune.

Nancy had found Joanna's gold!

14

Thieves on the Run

Nancy fingered the precious gold necklace, then ran her hand through the rest of the gleaming objects in the box. "I can't believe it," she murmured. "I found it! I found the Atwood fortune! I can't wait to show it to Joanna!"

Nancy knew that would have to wait. She still had three thieves to catch, and every second counted. She just hoped they were still in River Heights. Ethan had been talking about taking a "little vacation." They might be leaving town at this very instant.

Quickly Nancy replaced the gold necklace in the wooden box, closed the lid, and pressed the false bottom of the coffin back into position. She'd come back and get it after the thieves were caught. It would stay safely tucked away in its hiding place until then.

Now Nancy was ready to go after Ethan, Holly, and Kristin. The trouble was, where should she look for them? They could be anywhere in River Heights—or beyond it by now. Nancy was certain that if she could find the stolen goods, she'd find the thieves, too. After all, it would take them a long time to pack up all the loot and get out of town.

Maybe they'd left a clue in the mausoleum. One quick look around the place couldn't hurt.

Nancy walked around the marble tomb, but she soon realized that the place had been cleaned out. There was nothing on the stark stone floor. The tomb's strange carvings seemed to laugh at her from the walls.

Curiously, Nancy stepped closer to a little stone tree etched in the wall.

Suddenly she remembered that this was the spot where she, Bess, and George had entered the tomb the other day. As she gazed hard at the wall, she could just make out the shape of the door.

Nancy's eyes wandered back to the stone carving directly above the door. Of course! The carved tree marked this door, just the way the painted trees had marked the other secret doors! Could the other symbols mark other doors? Excited, Nancy wheeled around. The stone bird glared at her from across the room.

Wait a minute, Nancy thought. That's not just any kind of bird. It's a rooster—a rooster like the ones on the door knocker and weather vane at Joanna's house. It was a good bet that there was a second door beneath the bird, one leading straight to the Williamses' house.

But what about the third and last carving—the dragon? She stared at it closely. Of course! That was the dragon on her half of the map, only here it wasn't breathing fire. But it was definitely the dragon that had marked the Mortmain mansion!

Suddenly everything fell into place for Nancy. It made perfect sense that there'd be a secret passageway under the Mortmain house, too. And it explained how Holly, Ethan, and Kristin had found their way to the Mortmain mansion, even though it was marked on Nancy's half of the map.

They'd probably broken into the mausoleum and seen the carving of the tree. They had matched that tree with the one on their part of the map. Then they'd stumbled on the secret doors and found the three passageways. The one with the dragon would have led them right to the Mortmain mansion. Nancy hadn't discovered that passageway when she was at the house because the cellar door had been locked. She'd never had a chance to get into the basement.

But there was no reason for the thieves to keep the basement door locked unless they were storing the stolen goods down there.

Suddenly Nancy was sure that was where she'd find Ethan, Holly, and Kristin—at the Mortmain mansion, packing up their stolen goods in order to get out of River Heights. Well, they wouldn't get away. Nancy was going to stop them cold.

She knew she couldn't face them alone. She needed help. A couple of police officers would do just perfectly. All she had to do was get to a phone and call the station.

There wasn't a moment to lose. Nancy hurried to the coffin. She climbed into it, balancing her feet on the edge. Then she pulled herself quickly out of the mausoleum through the skylight. Ignoring the rain, she ran as fast as she could through the cemetery to Joanna's house. I hope the Williamses are home by now, Nancy thought as she hammered on the door with her hand. After all, she *had* told them to stay away tonight, in order to leave the house empty for the robbery setup. It would be awful if, after all this, Joanna wasn't home so Nancy couldn't call the police.

Finally Joanna came to the door. "Nancy!" she exclaimed. "What's going on? You're soaking wet."

"We're going to lose the thieves!" Nancy explained hastily. "Unless we act *now!*" Joanna stared at her openmouthed as Nancy ran past her to the phone.

"Police department," the precinct operator

answered. It wasn't the person who usually picked up the phone at the department.

"Hi, this is Nancy Drew. I'd like to speak to Chief McGinnis, please. Or Officer Marquez, Caplan, or Pierce," she added, naming the officers who had been on the two stakeouts.

"I'm sorry, Ms. Drew. The chief went home an hour ago. And the other officers are out on duty. What's the problem?"

Quickly Nancy explained the whole situation, including the sting operation she'd set up with the chief. She could tell from the silence on the other end of the line that the operator wasn't sure whether to believe her or not.

"Look, I'll take your number, and when the sergeant's free, I'll have him call you," the operator told Nancy.

"But—" Nancy began.

"I'm sorry, Ms. Drew," interrupted the operator. "I have a radio call coming in. Please give me a number where you can be reached."

Nancy left Joanna's number with the police operator, then pushed the redial button and punched George's phone number. The phone rang half a dozen times before a man's voice answered it. "Hello?" George's father said sleepily.

"Hi, Mr. Fayne, it's Nancy. Sorry to call so late, but I've got to talk to George right away."

"I'll get her," replied Mr. Fayne. "I think she's still up."

Nancy heard Mr. Fayne put down the receiver. A moment later, George's voice came over the phone. "Nancy? What's up?" she said.

"I need you to help me catch a couple of crooks," Nancy told her. She quickly explained the situation to George.

After George had gotten over her surprise that the thieves were Ethan, Holly, and Kristin, she said, "Just tell me what you want me to do."

"Remember the old Mortmain mansion? Get over there as soon as possible. Park your car down the block from the house. I'll meet you at the foot of the driveway. And call Bess, too."

"Right," said George. "Bess and I will meet you there in ten minutes."

Nancy hung up the phone.

"What's going on, Nancy?" asked Joanna. She was standing in the doorway of the living room.

"I can't explain now," Nancy replied. "But if the police call here, would you tell them to send a squad car over to the Mortmain mansion? And may I borrow your car?" Joanna nodded, quickly pulled the keys from her purse, and handed them over. "I'll be back— soon, I hope," Nancy told her. "And then I'll show you the gold. I found it!"

Joanna gasped in astonishment. Nancy flashed her a big smile, then hurried out of the house to the car. At least the rain had finally

131

stopped. As she headed toward the Mortmain mansion, she couldn't help worrying. Ethan, Holly, and even Kristin were tougher than they'd seemed. Ethan and Holly had attempted to bury her alive. If Nancy showed up at the mansion, they might try to get rid of her again. And maybe this time they'd succeed.

"Hey, that's my family's silver coffee pot," Bess whispered indignantly. She and George were standing at the open back doors of a large light blue van that was packed half full with boxes. The box containing the Marvins' coffee pot was near the rear, its flap open.

Nancy was crouching beside the van, checking its tires. "The treads match the tracks we found," she said. "Now I know for sure that this is the truck Ethan and his friends used during the robberies."

"They must be loading it up to get out of town," George put in.

"Well, we're going to make sure they stay in River Heights!" Nancy said firmly.

"What's the plan?" asked George.

"We'll hide behind the van," Nancy explained. "When they come out of the house with their arms full of stolen goods, we'll nail them."

"Nancy—" Bess began in a worried voice. But there was no time for her to finish. The heavy door of the Mortmain mansion was creaking open.

"Quick, hide!" Nancy whispered.

As she and her friends hurried around the van, Nancy saw Ethan and Kristin coming down the weedy walkway, struggling under the weight of a computer and its printer.

"What do you think's happening inside the coffin now?" Kristin was asking uncertainly.

"Nancy Drew's probably running out of air," Ethan replied with a harsh laugh.

Just then, Nancy saw Holly come out of the house. She was carrying a large cardboard box. Good, thought Nancy. They'd be able to catch all three of them together.

Ethan took a few more steps toward the van. By now he was close enough for Nancy to grab him. It was too good a chance to miss. "Go!" she shouted, signaling her friends to move. In a flash, she'd jumped up behind Ethan and thrown her arms around his chest. The computer spilled out of his grasp and crashed to the ground.

"Hey!" Ethan yelled in surprise.

Out of the corner of her eye, Nancy saw Kristin drop the printer and begin to back away. Then the younger girl sat down on the sidewalk and began to cry. Bess and George were holding on to Holly.

Suddenly, before Nancy had time to react,

Ethan tore her hands away from his chest. He whirled around and grabbed her arm tightly. With his free hand, he reached into his pocket and pulled out his knife.

He glared at Nancy. "I don't know how you got out of that coffin," he said to her, "but I do know one thing. You've interfered in my business for the last time."

15

The Police Step In

"You can't get away with this," Nancy said evenly. "Why don't you just let me go?"

Ethan ignored her. "Tell your friends to leave Holly alone," he said to Nancy. When she didn't say anything, he tightened his grip on her arm. "Do it!" he shouted.

Nancy hesitated for a moment. Then she said, "Bess, George, let Holly go."

"Smart girl," Ethan said, loosening his grip a little. "I like to have my orders obeyed."

"So I've noticed," muttered Nancy.

Bess and George released Holly. Instantly, she ran over to Ethan. "Get into the van," Ethan told her.

"What about Kristin?" Holly asked, motioning toward the younger girl.

Ethan looked at Kristin, who was still sitting on the sidewalk, sobbing. He sighed and said,

"It's really too bad she's never gotten the message that crime really does pay."

"No, it doesn't," said a man's gruff voice. "Drop the weapon, Davidson. My partner and I have you covered." A tall police officer stepped out of the shadows. He had his revolver trained on Ethan. Instantly, Ethan released his grip on Nancy.

"Officer Marquez!" Nancy cried as she recognized the police officer. "Am I glad to see you! I was sure the police department had deserted us on this one."

"Actually, I hate to tell you this, Nancy, but we almost did." Marquez worked efficiently, snapping handcuffs on Ethan as he talked. Meanwhile, his partner was taking care of Holly.

"Whoever was screaming in the graveyard led me on a wild-goose chase. It took me a long time to get back to the cemetery, and when I did, you were gone. That didn't sit too well with me—you didn't seem like the type to give up—but there was nothing I could do about it."

"How did you find us?" Nancy wanted to know. She walked over to Kristin and led her over to where the other police officer was holding Ethan and Holly. Marquez's partner handcuffed Kristin. Then he ushered the three thieves into the backseat of the patrol car.

"When I got back to the station, the police

operator gave me your message," Marquez told Nancy. "I called the number you left, and Mrs. Williams told me where you'd gone. So my partner and I came right over here."

"Well, you were just in time," Nancy told him. "If you two hadn't shown up, we would have lost those crooks for sure."

She led the officer to the van and showed him the stolen goods crammed in the back. "I've got a hunch there's a whole lot more stuff like this in the basement of the mansion," she told Marquez.

"Let's check it out," Officer Marquez replied, removing a flashlight from his belt. He turned to his partner. "Walt, you stay here with the alleged thieves. The rest of you, come on!"

Nancy led the police officer and her friends through the mansion to the basement door. Since Ethan, Holly, and Kristin hadn't quite finished moving all the loot out, the door stood wide open. The four of them headed down the stairs.

"Wow!" George exclaimed as she stared at the huge pile of stolen goods. "Look at all that stuff!" Half a dozen TVs stood in a jumbled mound, along with items of clothing, records, jewelry, a couple of paintings, and even a silver tea set.

"I just hope my other earring is in there somewhere," Bess said with a sigh.

"I've seen enough," Officer Marquez said.

"I'll head back to the station now to make a full report and call off the stakeout at the cabin."

"Right, Officer," said Nancy. "And thanks for getting here so fast."

"Thanks for catching the thieves. That was great detective work," Marquez called out as he headed back up the stairs.

Nancy turned and began to look around the basement.

"Look!" she exclaimed. A drawing of a dragon breathing fire had been painted on the rough basement wall. Beneath it, another secret door stood open. "That's got to be the third passageway—the one leading to the mausoleum," she said to her friends.

Nancy smiled. "And speaking of the Mortmain mausoleum, there's something pretty incredible in that weird old tomb that I want to show you."

"When can we see it?" George asked excitedly.

"How about right now?" Nancy replied. "We'll get it and take it to Joanna and Josh."

Bess groaned. "But, Nancy," she complained, "it's the middle of the night. We can't wake those two up now. Josh must have been asleep for hours and Joanna has to go to work early tomorrow."

"I have to return her car anyway, but I think she'll want to stay up to see this," Nancy said, her eyes twinkling mischievously. "In fact, after tonight, Joanna will probably be able to quit her job.''

"Nancy," George said suspiciously, "are you trying to tell me that you've found the missing fortune?''

"That's right! Come on, guys. Let's go give Joanna and Josh that gold!''

An hour later Nancy, Bess, and George were seated in Joanna's kitchen. They'd gone back to the tomb, carefully removed the box of gold from its hiding place, and given it to the Williamses.

Joanna was thrilled to see the gold. "Nancy, I can't believe you found it!'' she said happily. She bent toward the open box, running her fingers through the fortune in jewelry that now belonged to her. The tired circles under her eyes that Nancy had noticed a few days before seemed magically to have disappeared.

Josh stifled a yawn, then casually picked out a heavy gold bracelet. "Here, Mommy," he said. "Wear this. It's pretty.''

Joanna laughed as she slipped the shining bracelet around her wrist. "Nancy, you've changed our lives," she said. "I want to thank you for everything you've done for us. And this is the best way I can think of to show my gratitude." She began to rummage around in the box.

"Joanna, you don't have to give me anything," Nancy protested. "That's not why I helped you."

"Nonsense," Joanna countered. "I want to, and so does Josh."

As Joanna felt toward the bottom of the box, her expression suddenly changed. Her mouth rounded into a surprised "Oh!" When she took her hand out of the box, she wasn't holding a necklace or a pendant. Instead, she held a leather-bound book. Gold-embossed letters on the outside read, "Diary Journal."

Bess peered over Joanna's shoulder. "That looks a lot like *my* diary, only older. Let's see what's written in it."

George smiled at her cousin and rolled her eyes. "Sometimes I really can't believe you, Bess. You're interested in gossip even if it *is* ancient history!"

"Actually, this diary might be really important," Nancy put in. "It could help us clear up a couple of mysteries that are still bothering me. Like why were all these secret passageways and this empty tomb built in the first place? How did Laura Atwood find out about them in order to hide her gold here? And why did she leave her fortune to the Williamses?"

Joanna nodded. "I'd like to have the answer to that last question for sure. After all, Josh and I had never even heard of Laura Atwood before the lawyer called us."

Nancy reached out and touched the diary's

140

rich leather cover. "I'm sure this holds the key," she said. "But I don't think I should be the one to read it. Whoever put it in here left it for the person who would eventually own the gold—as a kind of explanation. Why don't you take it, Joanna? You're the one who really deserves the answers."

Joanna beamed at her. "I'm so excited, I think I'll spend the whole night reading this little book. Come and see me tomorrow. I'll tell all!"

16

Bethany's Story

"I read the entire diary last night from cover to cover," Joanna told Nancy, Bess, and George the next evening. "I stayed up all night and watched the sunrise this morning just after I finished." Joanna picked up the ancient leather-bound diary that had been lying on the kitchen table.

"It tells an amazing story—I couldn't put the book down." She leaned over the table and poured iced tea into tall glasses.

"What does it say?" asked Bess. She was sitting at the table with Josh on her lap.

"The story begins well over a hundred years ago, with a woman named Bethany Mortmain. She's the one who wrote the diary, and it's her story I'm going to tell. It was back in those terrible days when slavery still existed in this country, when black people like Josh and me couldn't live free wherever we wanted."

Joanna handed a glass of iced tea to each girl. Then she gave Josh a glass of orange juice.

"Bethany was a white woman, a rich elderly widow and a good woman," Joanna continued. "She was opposed to slavery, and she decided to do something about it. She used her money to set up one of the most important stations on the Underground Railroad in this part of the country."

"The Underground Railroad?" Bess exclaimed. "I remember learning about that in history class."

"That's right," Nancy put in. "It was a special network of people who helped slaves escape to freedom in the northern states and Canada. The slaves would travel at night to avoid the people who were trying to capture them. During the day they hid in people's houses—they used to call these people station masters."

"The slaves didn't always make it to freedom," George added, "and when they didn't, it was awful. After a special law was passed, slave owners could even come up here to the North to catch runaway slaves."

Joanna nodded. "Bethany Mortmain was one of the people who helped slaves make it to freedom and *stay* free. She used her money to build a complex system of tunnels and secret hiding places—all those places Nancy discovered in the past few days. Because her Underground Railroad station was so safe, she helped hundreds to freedom.

"One of the people she helped was my great-great-grandmother Tula. By the time Tula reached River Heights, she was frightened, exhausted, and just plain sick. Bethany nursed her back to health, and the two women became friends—really special friends.

"Anyway," Joanna continued, "by the time Tula was well enough to leave, the Underground station was very busy. And the slave catchers were beginning to suspect Bethany. It was too much for one woman to handle. Without help, Bethany might have had to close the station, and that would have left many escaping slaves in danger.

"Well, Tula refused to let that happen. She stayed on to help Bethany."

"But wasn't Tula herself in danger?" Bess wanted to know. "Couldn't the slave catchers have hunted her down and sent her back to the slave states in the South?"

Joanna nodded. "Yes, but she knew her work here was important—more important than her own life, even."

"What a brave woman!" George exclaimed.

Nancy glanced at her friends. She noticed that their glasses were standing untouched on the kitchen table. Both were fascinated by the story Joanna had read in Bethany Mortmain's diary.

Joanna continued. "Eventually, a man named Elias Ward came through the station, and he and Tula fell in love. Soon they were married. Within a few days, Tula and her new husband left for Toronto, Canada, to settle down and start a family in freedom. It was hard for her and Bethany to say goodbye, but they had to do it. They knew they might never see each other again.

"In time, the two friends lost touch. Bethany didn't know where Tula had settled, and Tula never returned to River Heights."

"That's really sad," Nancy said.

"Anyway, Bethany wanted to send Tula some money. She knew that as escaped slaves, she and her husband would probably be very poor. But she could never find them. She did write into her will that if Tula's family could ever be found, they should share any inheritance equally with her own children."

"And the gold?" Nancy asked. "How did that come to be hidden?"

"People had trouble with thieves breaking into houses, even in those days. There had been a rash of robberies in Bethany's neighborhood. She was afraid her house would be broken into, so she hid the bulk of her wealth in the mausoleum, where she had hidden escaping slaves. By that time Bethany was a very sick woman, and she knew she didn't have long to live. She made a map and tore it in two so that only her heirs would be able to find the gold—but obviously they never did. The gold—and the diary, which she left as an explanation of the whole story—stayed in the box until yesterday, when Nancy discovered it."

"Wow!" Nancy exclaimed. "Then that jewelry had been there for over a hundred years! But where does Laura Atwood come into all this? And how did she find out about the hidden gold?"

"Laura was Bethany's descendant. She was born Laura Mortmain. And she knew about the gold, from stories passed down over the years from relative to relative. She didn't know where the gold and the map were hidden, just that a story about them existed from long ago.

"Laura had also heard family stories about her great-grandmother's dying wish—that her friend Tula Ward finally receive the money. Since Laura was an only child and she and her husband had no children, she decided to fulfill her great-grandmother's desire and leave everything, including the gold, to Tula's descendants. Her lawyer traveled to Toronto and looked up the Wards and their descendants in the department of records. That's how he found Josh and me."

"And Laura Atwood didn't reveal any of this family history in her will?" Nancy asked.

Joanna shook her head. "I think she wanted me to find out for myself."

Bess sighed. "How romantic. A friendship that survives a hundred years later, even after both women are long dead."

"It's a beautiful story," Nancy agreed.

"Yes, it is," Joanna said. "And all this has come to pass thanks to a modern-day friendship—the friendship you three have given Josh and me." She smiled at them. Then she slipped Nancy, Bess, and George each a small package wrapped in rainbow-colored paper.

Nancy unwrapped the package carefully. A chain of golden flowers held together by finely crafted gold leaves fell into her hand. "Oh, Joanna, it's *gorgeous*," Nancy said breathily. She held it up to her neck. "But it's too generous. I can't take it."

"Of course you can," Joanna told her. "There's plenty left for Josh and me—and I want you to have the necklace as a memento of the friendship between Bethany and Tula." She reached over and clasped the precious necklace behind Nancy's neck. "It looks beautiful on you," Joanna said, smiling.

"Thank you, Joanna," Nancy said warmly. "I'll treasure this necklace always."

Bess received a beautiful bracelet and

George, a pair of drop earrings. Both of them thanked Joanna sincerely.

Then Joanna asked Nancy, "What happened to those three thieves you caught?"

"And what happened to the other part of the map?" Bess put in.

Nancy shook her shining hair, her new necklace jingling delicately as she did. "I talked to Chief McGinnis this morning. He said the police found the map piece in the glove compartment of Ethan's van. The chief also told me that Ethan and Holly are being charged with robbery, possession of a weapon, and attempted murder. Kristin will probably get off with probation."

"She ought to be more careful next time she chooses her friends," George said.

"What about the Rollinses?" Bess wanted to know.

"The Rollinses have been completely cleared of the robberies," Nancy continued. "They finally came forward and told the police they had been visiting Francesca Rollins's sick mother in California all this time. The police were able to verify their story."

"Anyway," Nancy went on, "we know more about what happened now that Ethan, Kristin, and Holly have made their statements to the police. As you know, Kristin found the map half in the wardrobe her mother bought from Joanna. She showed it to Ethan and Holly, who explored the area and found the hidden passages. Once they discovered the mausoleum, it was easy to find the other hidden corridors because all of them led directly to the tomb."

"Right. It was easier for them than for you," George commented.

"Anyway, once Ethan and Holly saw the ready-made escape routes leading all over the area, they cooked up the plan to use the passageways as a getaway system for a rash of neighborhood robberies. It worked pretty well, too."

"Until you showed up," George said.

"Well, actually, I didn't suspect a thing at first. In fact, those three thought I knew a lot more than I did, just because I happened to be in the cemetery that first night. And then, when I showed up at the Curious Cat, they were sure I was on to them. Kristin flipped when she saw me looking through the wardrobe and asking her mother about it. She called Ethan and followed his instruction to leave a threatening note on my car."

"It must have driven them crazy," Bess exclaimed. "The more often they ran into you, the more certain they became that you were on to them."

"So they broke into your house as a second warning," Joanna put in.

Nancy nodded. "And I guess that night we heard sounds in Joanna's basement, Ethan,

Holly, and Kristin were moving stolen goods into a safer passageway," Bess said.

"Right," Nancy replied. She grinned at Bess. "But we scared them off."

"And now," George said, "thanks to your hard work, you and Bess's family and all the other robbery victims will get their property back."

"And Joanna and Josh get their rightful inheritance," George added.

Joanna picked up her glass of iced tea. "More important than that, we've recovered a fascinating piece of our family's history—and made three wonderful friends in the process."

"I guess this whole case really has been about friendship," Nancy mused. "About Bethany and Tula's friendship. About my friendships with all of you."

"Well, I'm all for friendship," Joanna replied with a smile. "So I'd like to propose a toast." She lifted her glass of iced tea high in the air, and Nancy and her friends quickly did the same. "Here's to Tula and Bethany, and a friendship that's lasted for over a hundred years. And here's to Nancy, Bess, and George. May their friendship last just as long!"

Nancy smiled happily as she lifted her glass of iced tea to her lips. It was the perfect toast.

THE HARDY BOYS® SERIES By Franklin W. Dixon

☐ #59: NIGHT OF THE WEREWOLF	70993-3/$3.50	
☐ #60: MYSTERY OF THE SAMURAI		
SWORD	67302-5/$3.99	
☐ #61: THE PENTAGON SPY	67221-5/$3.99	
☐ #62: THE APEMAN'S SECRET	69068-X/$3.50	
☐ #63: THE MUMMY CASE	64289-8/$3.99	
☐ #64: MYSTERY OF SMUGGLERS COVE	66229-5/$3.50	
☐ #65: THE STONE IDOL	69402-2/$3.50	
☐ #66: THE VANISHING THIEVES	63890-4/$3.99	
☐ #67: THE OUTLAW'S SILVER	74229-9/$3.50	
☐ #68: DEADLY CHASE	62477-6/$3.50	
☐ #69: THE FOUR-HEADED DRAGON	65797-6/$3.50	
☐ #70: THE INFINITY CLUE	69154-6/$3.50	
☐ #71: TRACK OF THE ZOMBIE	62623-X/$3.50	
☐ #72: THE VOODOO PLOT	64287-1/$3.99	
☐ #73: THE BILLION DOLLAR		
RANSOM	66228-7/$3.50	
☐ #74: TIC-TAC TERROR	66858-7/$3.50	
☐ #75: TRAPPED AT SEA	64290-1/$3.50	
☐ #76: GAME PLAN FOR DISASTER	72321-9/$3.50	
☐ #77: THE CRIMSON FLAME	64286-3/$3.99	
☐ #78: CAVE IN	69486-3/$3.50	
☐ #79: SKY SABOTAGE	62625-6/$3.50	
☐ #80: THE ROARING RIVER		
MYSTERY	73004-5/$3.50	
☐ #81: THE DEMON'S DEN	62622-1/$3.50	
☐ #82: THE BLACKWING PUZZLE	70472-9/$3.50	
☐ #83: THE SWAMP MONSTER	49727-8/$3.50	
☐ #84: REVENGE OF THE DESERT		
PHANTOM	49729-4/$3.50	
☐ #85: SKYFIRE PUZZLE	67458-7/$3.50	
☐ #86: THE MYSTERY OF THE		
SILVER STAR	64374-6/$3.50	
☐ #87: PROGRAM FOR DESTRUCTION	64895-0/$3.99	
☐ #88: TRICKY BUSINESS	64973-6/$3.99	
☐ #89: THE SKY BLUE FRAME	64974-4/$3.50	
☐ #90: DANGER ON THE DIAMOND	63425-9/$3.99	

☐ #91: SHIELD OF FEAR	66308-9/$3.50	
☐ #92: THE SHADOW KILLERS	66309-7/$3.99	
☐ #93: THE SERPENT'S TOOTH		
MYSTERY	66310-0/$3.50	
☐ #94: BREAKDOWN IN AXEBLADE	66311-9/$3.50	
☐ #95: DANGER ON THE AIR	66305-4/$3.50	
☐ #96: WIPEOUT	66306-2/$3.50	
☐ #97: CAST OF CRIMINALS	66307-0/$3.50	
☐ #98: SPARK OF SUSPICION	66304-6/$3.99	
☐ #99: DUNGEON OF DOOM	69449-9/$3.50	
☐ #100: THE SECRET OF ISLAND		
TREASURE	69450-2/$3.50	
☐ #101: THE MONEY HUNT	69451-0/$3.50	
☐ #102: TERMINAL SHOCK	69288-7/$3.50	
☐ #103: THE MILLION-DOLLAR		
NIGHTMARE	69272-0/$3.99	
☐ #104: TRICKS OF THE TRADE	69273-9/$3.50	
☐ #105: THE SMOKE SCREEN		
MYSTERY	69274-7/$3.99	
☐ #106: ATTACK OF THE		
VIDEO VILLIANS	69275-5/$3.99	
☐ #107: PANIC ON GULL ISLAND	69276-3/$3.99	
☐ #108: FEAR ON WHEELS	69277-1/$3.99	
☐ #109: THE PRIME-TIME CRIME	69278-X/$3.50	
☐ #110: THE SECRET OF SIGMA SEVEN	72717-6/$3.99	
☐ #111: THREE-RING TERROR	73057-6/$3.99	
☐ #112: THE DEMOLITION MISSION	73058-4/$3.99	
☐ #113: RADICAL MOVES	73060-6/$3.99	
☐ #114: THE CASE OF THE		
COUNTERFEIT CRIMINALS	73061-4/$3.99	
☐ #115: SABOTAGE AT SPORTS CITY	73062-2/$3.99	
☐ #116: ROCK 'N' ROLL RENEGADES	73063-0/$3.99	
☐ #117: THE BASEBALL CARD CONSPIRACY	73064-9/$3.99	
☐ #118: DANGER IN THE FOURTH DIMENSION	79308-X/$3.99	
☐ #119: TROUBLE AT COYOTE CANYON	79309-8/$3.99	
☐ #120: CASE OF THE COSMIC KIDNAPPING	79310-1/$3.99	
☐ THE HARDY BOYS GHOST STORIES	69133-3/$3.50	

NANCY DREW® MYSTERY STORIES By Carolyn Keene